Youth Sports:
start here...

Everything You Need to Know About Promoting Health and Preventing Injury for Your Young Athlete

by Julie A. Buckley, MD, and
Eugene Monroe, Baltimore Raven

Designer Credits
Cover art by Sally Eckhoff
Interior design by Typeflow
Interior Illustrations by Sally Eckhoff

From Healthy You Books, an imprint of Water Street Press,
in association with the Healthy U Now Foundation.

Produced in the USA

ISBN-13: 978-1-62134-200-7

Library of Congress Control Number: 2016934004

Disclaimer: Our purpose in writing *Youth Sports: Start Here* is to provide
parents with information that will empower them, their children, and
their physician to make better healthcare decisions. The content of
this book cannot replace a physician's opinion and is not intended
to be used to make a diagnosis or to recommend a treatment. We
recommend you use this information as you consult with your physician
with respect to your medical history and unique circumstances.

For my father, the first football player I ever knew. Without your answer to my question "Daddy, what's a punt?" this book might not have come into being.

For my personal Toto, who pulled back the curtain, and showed me the true Wizard. No matter how loudly the Great and Powerful Oz bellows for me to pay no attention, I cannot un-see the man behind the curtain!

~Julie

To Nureya… you enhance me in every way imaginable and make me perfect in my shortcomings.

~Eugene

Acknowledgments

JULIE

Working with professional athletes has been one of the most illuminating aspects of my work as a physician. The joy and pride I experience knowing that "I helped!" as they do their jobs better and healthier — as a result of our time together — is boundless. To each and every one of them, I say thank you from the bottom of my heart.

To Lynn Vannucci, all things writing and publishing in my world, thank you for the gift of your words and your endless patience.

To the team that makes up Water Street Press — thank you for your help in making the machine run. In a world of fast-paced electronic everything, it's easy to forget that there are always real-life people operating keyboards and smart phones!

To my family, who make a sacrifice greater than anyone will ever know so that I can try to send a little more light out there into a world that so desperately needs a little illuminating.

To Tony and Michelle Pashos — you were the first, and you changed our family's life forever. We miss you daily.

There are quite a few athletes who have crossed the threshold of our home and ventured into my family's life and our hearts. We have danced, sung, played piano, eaten, celebrated, put angels onto Christmas trees, shopped, cooked, traveled, hugged, moved, cried, laughed and loved. No words can express my gratitude for your coming into our lives — I am an abundantly joy-filled mother and grandmother so many more times over than I ever thought I would be.

EUGENE

I proudly say thank you to…

My Lord, Jesus Christ, for constructing my life in a way that is a living and walking testimony of His divine power and grace. In addition to blessing me with a tremendous capacity to work, he has provided me with precious souls who have guided me to success in many different areas.

My mother, for her love and endurance. Together we persevered through tough times, all with love, which ultimately molded the clay of the man and father I am becoming daily.

Uncle Eugene, for becoming my father figure after my dad's passing and guiding me with wise words and consistency.

Frank Colabella, for being a father figure, guidance counselor, trainer, and best friend.

Robin Crudup and Sharon White, the mothers of my best friends, for becoming my loving mothers as well.

Aunt Susan, who I also call Mother, for being there as a protector and source of knowledge from the moment you walked into my life.

My children, Farah and Xavier, who are gifts from my Lord. I love you. You have forever changed my understanding of love, and no matter where life takes us, you have given me a purpose.

Dr. Julie Buckley, who has forever changed my life and my approach to health, and therefore my family's health and wellness destiny. Thank you for welcoming my family into yours.

This list is short, but the list of people who have positively impacted my life is long. For all of those who have gone unnamed here, please know that I'm forever grateful you have been a part of my journey, and I look forward to continuing the journey with all of you at my side.

Contents

Foreword:
Daddy First

MAURICE JONES-DREW

When I sat down to write the foreword for this book, I was torn about what voice I should use. Should I speak from the perspective of a professional athlete, as running back for the Jacksonville Jaguars and Oakland Raiders — the part of my life most readers will know me for? In a book about sports health, that seems, at first thought, to be the natural choice. The toll that playing sports can take on a human body is, after all, a subject about which I can speak with unquestioned authority.

But I've also got a lot of knowledge about how to take control of your health as an athlete. That's because, when I was playing for the Jags, I met Dr. Julie Buckley, the co-author of this book, who practices in Jacksonville, Florida. She's a passionate proponent of functional medicine, and she gave me so many practical and effective tools to use to heal when I was injured — as well as so many I could use to prevent injury in the first place. I know you have this book in your hands because you want to know what those tools are, too; in that case, should I write from the perspective of being Julie's patient?

I could also write as Eugene's friend and former teammate. He and I played together for the Jags and, over those years, we not only took the field together, we recognized that we were both on the same quest to sustain our health so that, when we left the NFL, we would do so in the best physical and mental shape possible.

But at the end of the day, this is a book about *youth sports* — a book that helps parents to help their kids stay healthy and injury-free while playing soccer and basketball and football, tennis and gymnastics, ballet and wresting, and any other physical activity their kids decide to do. I've been an advocate for youth for a long time. The Maurice Jones-Drew Foundation has been a partner with Wolfson's Children's Hospital in Jacksonville, Florida, in helping to create unique healing environments for sick kids. We run the Backpack Give Away Project to help needy students in their scholastic endeavors by providing them backpacks filled with school supplies. Through the Maurice Jones-Drew Football Camp — a camp for both boys and girls! — we mentor underprivileged and at-risk youth to help them learn, through exercise, lectures, and other activities, the values of self-respect, responsibility, accountability, persistence and teamwork, and motivate them to stay in school.

I think, however, that it is as a father of three — my sons Maurice and Madden, and my daughter Alayah — I can speak most meaningfully to the readers of this book. As any father or mother can tell you, being a parent is hands-down the hardest and most rewarding role in life. Like all parents, the well being of my children is the first thing I think about every day. It is what I worry most about, pray most about, and what can keep me up at night. I want my kids to be active people who are passionately engaged in whatever it is that brings them joy — sports, school, the arts. I want them to be able to take full advantage of the opportunities they're offered. I want them to have the vibrant health that will allow them to work hard to fulfill their potential.

Because of the lessons I have learned working with Julie through many of the years of my professional career, I rest easy knowing I have the knowledge and resources I need to help my own kids reach these goals.

So, speaking as one parent to another, the book you hold in your hands will help you to rest easy, too. You now own the book that will be your primary resource for raising healthy, active kids.

Maurice Jones-Drew
May 2015

Author's Note

JULIE A. BUCKLEY

Whether I'm talking about autism, breast cancer, or how to protect and heal young athletes (the subjects of my first three books), I approach health from the perspective of functional medicine. This means that, while each subject involves very specific problems, and solutions that are distinct to those problems, all three have in common the principles of functional medicine. If you have read my earlier books you will find brief overlaps of basic functional medicine information as well as certain science. The explanations of this basic information are tailored to my audience — in this book, for example, you'll find the science behind the prevention and healing of youth sports injuries laid out in a way that will help parents explain it to their young athletes.

I also want to take this opportunity to explain that, while I do have opinions regarding certain products and brands — opinions that I have expressed within these pages — neither my professional practice, my foundation, nor myself, personally, are affiliated in any financial way with those entities. And never will be. A physician must be unencumbered by any financial considerations relative to the health of her patients and making recommendations for treatment. I believe sponsorship in any form by a brand or a product has the potential to compromise a physician's ability to ethically determine a course of treatment and to make optimal individualized recommendations.

Thanks,
Julie A. Buckley, MD

Introduction:
Why would anyone in her right mind let her kid play football?

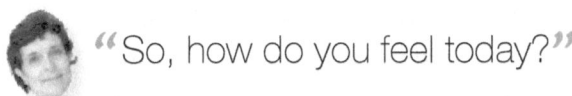 " So, how do you feel today? "

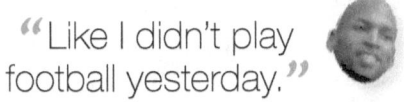 " Like I didn't play football yesterday. "

It was one of the best compliments I've ever received, the Monday I texted my friend and patient Eugene Monroe, then left tackle for the Jacksonville Jaguars, after a hard-hitting Sunday afternoon game and asked him how he felt. I swear I could hear the slow smile come across his face as I read his reply: "Like I didn't play football yesterday."

I can't take all the credit, of course, for how good Eugene was feeling that day — a day after he'd spent four consecutive hours knocking around a one-hundred-and-twenty-yard field with twenty-one other two-hundred-and-fifty-pound mountains of solid muscle, a day when he should have been feeling the way most other players feel after a game: bruised and battered, sore and stiff, achy, groggy and cranky. Indeed, I give most of the credit to Eugene himself — as his doctor, I may provide him with options he can take advantage of to understand, prevent,

1

and heal the injuries he will almost inevitably sustain on the field, but Eugene is the one with the self-discipline to put these options into practice. His vigorous self-discipline is, indeed, one of the primary reasons I asked him to co-author this book with me: I am a scientist who can write pages and pages and pages that contain advice about sports medicine, and cite the scientific studies that back it up, but Eugene is a living, breathing, walking, talking, laughing, loving husband, father, and professional athlete at the peak of health because he has intelligently and consistently followed the best medical advice and maintained a proactive wellness program throughout his professional football career. We are setting out to write a book that parents can use to help inspire their kids to stay healthy while playing youth sports, a book that provides Mom and Dad with practical and even fun tools that will help them get the kids engaged and empowered about their own health — and my question is: who do you think kids are going to listen to? A doctor going on about medical science, or medical science filtered through the acquired life wisdom of a famous NFL left tackle?

As a parent, I know how important it is to consider your sources when you present information to kids. One day my then-teenage son, Matthew, announced to his father and me, as we sat at a place called Sneakers — one of our favorite restaurants, that he was going to purchase a motorcycle. He was eighteen years old, and he'd saved the money for the vehicle himself, so we couldn't ban the purchase outright, only argue against it, but parental logic got us exactly nowhere. Neither was Matthew moved by his father's getting irritated about him not listening to our well-reasoned arguments or my getting frantic at the thought of my son riding around Florida on what I could think of only as a 'death machine'. What did move Matthew? Why does he now have a nice, solid truck rather than a Harley? Because I had an ace up my sleeve.

 "Matt says he's buying a motorcycle."

 "Where are you?"

 "Sneakers."

 "Be right there."

Twenty minutes later Eugene walked into the restaurant, slid into the booth next to Matt and slapped him upside the head — gently. "What is wrong with you? You are not buying a motorcycle!" Matt gave me a death stare across the table. "What," Eugene asked, "did you think she wasn't gonna tell me?"

I grant you that part of Eugene's credibility with Matthew is cultural — we all want to emulate our heroes and our son, like everyone else in the family, is a huge football fan. But another, and I think larger and deeper, part is that as a role model, Eugene is completely authentic. "Do as I say, not as I do" does not apply here — Eugene understands his health and how to maintain it from an intellectual perspective, and he is disciplined enough to put this understanding into practice on a day-to-day, game-to-game basis. Even better, Eugene totally gets why he, as an athlete, needs to take certain steps and precautions now to maintain his physical health and his intellect over the long term.

And he understands that the why really doesn't have much to do with his viability as a football player.

Years ago, down in the bowels of EverBank Field where the Jags' families, friends, and other close supporters gather to celebrate or console after a game, I ran into one of the team's retired players. This man was in his early forties, just a few years younger than I was at the time, a nice guy, and he'd been good at the game during his years with the team, but now, like so many other retired players, he was — to put it simply and accurately — crippled. He could hardly walk.

At the time I ran into him, I'd just started to work with some of the players, teaching them about functional medicine and wellness and how to preserve their health during the brief but intense few years they would be active in the hazardous career they'd chosen. As I watched the retired gladiator limp away, a light bulb started blinking in my brain: this is why I want to work with these young men! I am an avowed and enthusiastic football fan, totally into the thrill of the offense and the vigor defense requires — and totally aware of the price this thrill and vigor can exact from the men who play the game for my pleasure.

As a fan, I watch with millions of other fans every season as the players on my team throw their full and imposing weight at the opposing team to block a play, or crawl out from under thousand-pound pile-ups, or take a hit so hard a helmet flies off a head. I gasp when a player goes down and doesn't get right back up and — whether I'm in the stadium or watching the game from the comfort of my living room, whether the player is on my team or my rival's — I breathe a sigh of relief when at last he rises to his feet. And then I silently pray that the blow will result in nothing of significance to the player's health. From Joe Theismann's leg to Napoleon McCallum's knee, most of us fans remember, have heard about, or have watched on You-Tube the most gruesomely famous times when the players did not rise.

What is less apparent to us fans — and therefore less likely at the forefront of our consciousness — are the hidden but equally routine results of all those blocks and hits and pile-ups. The incidence of painful arthritis, for example, that is higher for retired NFL players than for any other portion of the male population due to the simple fact that NFL players deal more frequently and more repeatedly with more severe joint strain and injury during the course of their short careers than any of the rest of us will likely suffer in a lifetime.[1]

What never fails to absolutely astonish me, however, is the stunning lack of imagination (or overabundance of denial) that allows some folks to think that, though bodies are being broken, somehow the brain isn't being broken as well. We've known about boxers who suffer with *dementia pugilistica* (DP), a neurodegenerative disease caused by repeated concussive or sub-concussive blows, since 1928[2], after all. And DP is but a variant of chronic traumatic encephalopathy (CTE) that is these days so much at the forefront of sports news and NFL settlements. Indeed, fabled quarterback Brett Favre, whose wife Deanna wrote the foreword to my last book — *Breast Cancer: Start*

---

1 http://media.mgnetwork.com/ncn/pdf/101111_arthritis_football.pdf
2 http://jama.jamanetwork.com/article.aspx?articleid=260461

Here— is one of the more recent players to come forward to say he is suffering with memory loss, a symptom associated with CTE. He is, like so many others, wondering what toll concussions will take on his brain.[1]

How many players have or will get CTE? We don't know, because the research is woefully behind where it ought to be considering the severity of the diagnosis and how long experts have known that it is the possible — even probable — result of an NFL career. What we do know is that of the eighty-five brains donated for posthumous study to Boston University's Center for the Study of Traumatic Encephalopathy, thirty-five of them were the brains of football players — and *only one* of those football-player brains showed no signs of CTE.[2] We also know that brain scans are now revealing that living players are suffering from CTE.[3] The odds that one of our football heroes is doing irreparable damage to his brain as he entertains us on Monday nights are staggering. And with CTE come life-altering — sometimes life-ending — symptoms:

+ depression[4]— the suicide rate for former NFL players is six times the national average;[5]
+ poor judgment — 78% of former NFL players go bankrupt or experience severe financial difficulty within two years of their retirement, and one can't put all the blame for that on youthful excess or bad financial advice;[6]

---

1 http://abcnews.go.com/Health/brett-favre-latest-nfl-player-memory-loss/story?id=20681336

2 http://abcnews.go.com/Health/cte-degenerative-brain-disease-found-34-pro-football/story?id=17869457

3 http://espn.go.com/espn/otl/story/_/id/8867972/ucla-study-finds-signs-cte-living-former-nfl-players-first-time

4 http://www.nytimes.com/packages/pdf/sports/football/concussions-study-20070531.pdf

5 http://www.imperfectenjoyment.com/2012/05/seau-nfl-suicide/

6 http://sports.yahoo.com/nfl/blog/shutdown_corner/post/Why-do-so-many-NFL-players-go-bankrupt-?urn=nfl,190555

- relationship difficulties — the divorce rate in the NFL is somewhere between 60% and 80%.[7]

As a fan, how great would it be to watch the game without knowing this kind of stuff? Without knowing the cost of our entertainment?

As a doctor, how great was it that I knew *the game doesn't have to exact such a ridiculous cost* from the guys on the field? How thankful was I that I had been given the gift of being able to work with these guys, and help at least some of the players avoid the fate of being similarly broken at the end of their careers!

Let me be clear. I want the players who are my patients to have great careers. But when all is said and done, what I want most is for them to retain the physical ability to get down on the floor, without pain, and take joy in playing with their kids. I want them to retain the mental capacity to help their kids with their algebra homework. I want them to retain the emotional capacity that will allow them to still be married to the same person. It would be an added bonus if, in the bargain, they could keep their jobs longer, and do their jobs better, in the very short career that is professional sports.

So WHAT DOES all this have to do with *your* kids? Why should you, as a parent, be concerned about statistics that demonstrate what a ruthlessly violent sport professional football really is? For all your child's or my child's prowess on the field, it is extremely unlikely that the vast majority of our kids will have a career at the most elite level of sport — the NFL, the NBA, the Olympics.

---

7 http://www.nytimes.com/2009/08/09/sports/football/09marriage.html

You should be concerned because in the same study that revealed the brains of thirty-four out of thirty-five football players contained evidence of CTE, six of the posthumously-studied CTE-affected brains were those of young men who had played the sport at only the high school level.[1] Because football is not the only sport in which repeated blows to the head are a risk — think of the chances of a child getting hit with a hockey stick, or 'beaned' by a baseball. Think of soccer, a sport in which hitting the ball with your head is a skill you must master to play the game well.

And, now that I have thus directed your thoughts, your question might be, Why in God's name would anyone let his kid play football? Or soccer? Why would a parent allow her child to be on the gymnastics team or swing a tennis racket? Why play sports at all? Why would a doctor, like me — and one who started out as a pediatrician, at that — allow her own son to play football, as I indeed did?

For quite a few very solid reasons.

First, kids just plain need exercise. If they don't get the appropriate amount of exercise — and preferably in an outdoor setting — they gain weight, tend toward sedentary lifestyles, risk developing disease. Also, without the outlet of physical activity, they can become depressed or, conversely, bounce off the walls of your house so it makes you wonder why it is you wanted kids in the first place. It is just a basic truth that exercise is good for you — it awakens your nerves, gets your blood flowing, tones your muscles, grows your bones, feeds your cells with oxygen so your mind is alert and your body feels good and you're able to do good things with a go get 'em attitude.

Next, organized sports are good for kids because they need to develop the ability to work as a part of a team.

---

1 http://www.sciencedaily.com/releases/2012/12/121203112808.htm

Teamwork is a critical life skill — think about it: every relationship he will ever have for the rest of his life, from the one he will have with his boss to the one he will have with his wife, will require teamwork for success. How to flourish as part of a team is one of the most important lessons we teach our kids.

Then there's the whole self-discipline angle. Participating in youth sports helps our kids develop the crucial ability to work hard toward the pursuit of a goal, whether that goal is swimming a second faster than the kid in the next lane, shooting baskets with more accuracy, or simply making the team in the first place. A child who has learned the habit of self-discipline through sports can also apply what he has learned in the classroom and it will be easier for him to be disciplined about his studies. And there's one more important advantage you give a kid by getting her involved in sports teams: this kid has less unstructured time than kids who don't play sports, but she has to maintain her grades in order to continue to play, so she's going to learn at a young age how to control her free time and use it efficiently and productively.

We also shouldn't overlook the benefits our kids get when they *lose* a game. Sure, participating in sports is a competitive undertaking — that's why they keep score, for heaven's sake! But learning about sportsmanship, and how to take a loss with grace — shaking hands with the winning team members when they come out on the short end — is a lesson that will serve them all their lives. Life, itself, won't always hand our kids the win — in fact, sometimes life's best lessons come from experiencing the loss, rather than the win. So teaching our children that it matters *how they play the game*— that if they play fair and to the best of their abilities they are never really losers — has value that extends far beyond the field or court or pitch. Losing with style is an art in and of itself, and one that our children deserve to possess.

Finally, but by no means of least importance, kids need to feel secure within community. Life, as we adults know all too well, is not, to put it mildly, wholly predictable. Introducing our children to groups in which they can find fellowship with other people who share their interests can provide the necessary, comforting sense of community and camaraderie that we humans crave. Church, Boy Scouts, film camp, pee-wee baseball, soccer, and swim team — and, yes, the football team — are all groups my kids have participated in, and where they have nurtured their sense of community. Being a part of a group that finds common purpose in rooting for the same college or pro sports team is another of those uplifting human communities.

The trick, then, is to help our kids participate wisely in youth sports. Allowing them to participate in, and *teaching them HOW to participate*— how to train and compete and be sportsmen and –women in the most thoughtful and proactive ways — can set them up with huge lifelong advantages.

IN THIS BOOK we'll discuss anatomy from a very specific point of view: a kid's. Growing a full-sized adult body is one of the hardest things a human being has to do in the course of a lifetime. We'll talk about the stresses — both good stresses and bad — that athletic activity puts on growing bones and joints and muscles.

We'll also focus on the brain — new research that helps us to understand the construction zone that is a child's brain (a construction zone that remains in flux at *least* until the child is in his or her early twenties, by the way), the ways the brain learns, how it can be injured while taking part in sports and, conversely, how important sports and other physical activity are to helping our kids maintain the mental edge they need to excel both athletically and scholastically.

We'll dive deeply into what functional medicine is, what its methods are and how critical they can be to helping both prevent and heal the injuries our kids will almost inevitably sustain as they participate in youth sports. And we'll offer tools that you, as a parent or guardian, can employ to help get your kid invested in her own health — while she is a young athlete, and for her whole life long.

Throughout this book you'll hear my voice presenting the science behind functional medicine and the methods you can employ to help your child, and you'll hear Eugene's voice speaking more directly to your kids, underscoring how he used the science in practical application. Think of this book as the ace up your sleeve.

Julie A. Buckley, MD
April 2015

I.

THE GROWING BODY

1

ALL KIDS DESERVE THE OPPORTUNITY TO EXCEL!

 *"* Growing a full-sized, adult body is one of the hardest things human beings have to do in the course of our lives. *"*

One of my young patients is a seventh grader named Nickie. Nickie is the goalie for her youth soccer team and she is so good at being a goalie that the Olympic people have already been around to watch her play and talk to her parents about her sports future. When I have taken care of a kid as long as I've taken care of Nickie — and taking care of Nickie goes back to the days before I started specializing in functional medicine, when I was still a typical, traditional pediatrician — I take a pride in their accomplishments that comes awfully close to the level of pride a parent takes. I don't think that's unusual. When you have known and worked with a child through so many years and stages of development, you become invested in her welfare in a way that is as maternal as it is medical. The child becomes one of your own, part of your tribe, a member of the extended family.

This is why I felt both compelled and free to speak to Nickie's parents with terrible frankness when I heard about the schedule she was keeping. In addition to the basic expectation that she would perform well in school and keep her grades up, Nickie was in regular training with her team seven days a week, playing in soccer tournaments for ten to seventeen weekends every year, and, on top of this, running a minimum of several miles four to five mornings a week.

I can't say this too often: **Growing a full-sized, adult body is one of the hardest things human beings have to do in the course of our lives. It is a task that takes an enormous amount of energy.** Therefore, we have to be incredibly careful about what we ask a child, a preteen, a teenager to accomplish in the course of a day that is in addition to her primary job, which is, simply and profoundly, *growing*.

This is a lesson I first learned not in medical school, while I was training to be a pediatrician, but first hand, and *as* a teenager. When I was in high school, I was busier than anyone should have a right to be. I kept my grades way up high (I hated getting things wrong on tests — a good thing when you want to head to med school), participated in competitive horseback riding, worked in the barn before school and before dinner seven days a week every week of the year, edited my high school yearbook, was a member of the high school varsity cheerleading squad, worked at the local hospital as an aide on the floors and a volunteer in the physical therapy department, did my household chores, babysat most weekends… It wasn't a surprise that I was tired all the time, but my mom was concerned about my level of energy — or, more accurately, she was concerned about my *lack* of energy. She took me to the family doctor to make sure there wasn't something organically wrong with me. Was I anemic? Did I need to have blood work?

No, the doctor told my mother and me, I was just too damned busy. "Julie," he asked, posing one of the more memorable questions I remember ever being directed at me, "do you have time to pick your nose?"

Excuse me?

Do you have time to sit and listen to your favorite record, or moon over your favorite rock star? To stare out the window for half an hour and daydream? To hit the snooze button, or even sleep in once in a while?

No, no, and absolutely not, I'd replied, and my doctor pointed out that then I had a big problem. He gave his prescription to my mother, "Mrs. Buckley, make sure this kid has at least some time every day set aside to pick her nose."

WE LIVE IN a wildly competitive culture. Our kids are challenged scholastically, athletically, and even socially every day, and we want ours to make the team, get into his first-choice school, win the prize, and rightly so — guiding our children to excellence is part of what being a parent is all about.

But overscheduling our kids — or letting them overschedule themselves, as I had done — can actually do more harm than good. And investing in a child's sports prowess above all other considerations can be downright dangerous. The reality television series *Friday Night Tykes* gives us a shocking example of the absolute nadir of the youth sports experience. A coach telling a ten-year-old boy to go on the field and hit another child so hard that "I don't care if he don't get up"? That's not just the wrong way to train young athletes, it truly is like watching televised child abuse.[1]

How do we find the balance between healthy involvement in sports and too much?

---

1 http://abcnews.go.com/GMA/video/friday-night-tykes-reality-show-fire-youth-football-22372651

A friend has a little boy. The kid plays baseball, and he's good at it. Mom is proud of her son's athletic achievements and Dad, who volunteers as the team's coach, is over the moon about them. As the kid continues to pitch no-hitters and hit homeruns, Dad admits to a little daydreaming about a major league career for junior. Still, Dad told me, "The day he tells me he doesn't want to play ball anymore, I'll be sad, but I'll support his decision. If he's not having fun on the ball field as a kid he's not going to have what it takes to play as an adult anyway. And he *is* a kid. I'm not going to ask him to pick the girl he wants to marry at age ten, so why would I ask him to pick his future career at that age?" The boy has also had enough time off the diamond to, in the last year, keep up his grades in school, construct a fort/treehouse in his backyard with his friends (having appropriated one dining room chair for building materials, but that's another story), and learn a little bit about physics (by building every rocker, glider, and boomerang in the amazing kids' book *The Flying Machine*[1]).

For me, this dad has a good handle on where the balance lies: supporting his son in a sport that gives them both pleasure, but being relaxed and realistic enough to allow the boy to find his own way — not pushing, not imposing his own ambitions on his son, but guiding and inspiring.

As we guide and inspire our own kids, perhaps the story of another young athlete can guide and inspire *us*.

---

1 http://www.amazon.com/Flying-Machine-Book-Helicopters-Boomerangs-ebook/dp/B0087GZEU0/ref=sr_1_1?s=books&ie=UTF8&qid=1405193010&sr=1-1&keywords=the+flying+machine

There's no way around it, I was an overweight, unathletic kid. My dad died when I was in the fifth grade, and though my mom always made sure I had enough food — enough *fuel*— to have played if I'd wanted to, she didn't know a lot about sports and so I didn't really think about them either. The emphasis was always on pushing me to excel in school. I was the kid who got straight A's — I'd get home from school, get my homework done, dream about what it would mean to be an engineer. Then I watched TV or played video games. I rarely went outside.

I started out doing martial arts, but I didn't do it because, at the time, it was, on its own, interesting to me. I did it because my older brother did it and I wanted to be like him. I tried playing basketball for one season, but I just didn't like the game very much. I was, however, a big kid — the biggest in my class, I think — and people were always sort of forcing me to try out for football. I was too big and heavy to play on the youth teams; I was big enough to have played with much older kids. But when I got to middle school I fit in enough to play with kids my own age. I was in sixth grade the first time I played football — and I was a natural, if only because at that level all you did was hit people. I was bigger and stronger than the other kids on the team so I hit better than the rest, and I started to have fun. I started to like football. Football changed my life.

I still consider myself an introvert, but playing ball pushed me out of my shell, it forced me to be more social. I learned self-discipline, teamwork, leadership — and these things filled me with a level of confidence that, even as an "A" student, I'd never had. I don't know where you learn these lessons except through sports.

I was fortunate in high school — I didn't suffer any injuries except a twisted ankle in my senior year. I had a good run playing offensive tackle for Plainfield High School in Plainfield, New Jersey, but there really wasn't a huge involvement at home in what I was doing. Then I got to college and that's where I started to take more of an interest in my health, mainly eating better because I wanted to shed a few pounds; it wasn't a serious lifestyle change.

Then, when it became real, that I had a legitimate chance of extending my football career to the NFL, I wanted to get my body working to its maximum potential. I knew enough to understand that what I ate, what I put inside of me, determined what I was able to put out in terms of my football performance. I didn't know much else about nutrition, however, so I relied on my training staff to steer me in the right direction. It's kind of crazy, though, how much there is to know about nutrition, and generally taking care of yourself, and how much even coaches and trainers don't know about how to help an athlete take good care of himself — even when taking care of himself means a better performance on the field of play. My wife, Nureya, jokes now that, at the time, we thought choosing to have dinner at the Boston Market was a healthier choice than eating at the local pizza parlor.

I'd been playing in the NFL for a year when I met Julie and got a whole new level of information. That's when the change in lifestyle really occurred. She helped me see that it wasn't all just about my last game. If I wanted to be a player who was valuable to my team, and have an extended career doing it, that was completely dependent on how healthy I was *inside*. How far you can run, how fast you can run, how much you can lift — it all comes down to how well you take care of yourself inside: the foods I ate and when I ate them, the supplements I took, the amount and quality of sleep I got, just to name a few things she schooled me about.

Now, as a father — my wife Nureya and I have two very young children, Farah, who is, as of this writing, three years old, and Xavier, who is nine months — I am certainly going to steer my kids into athletics. Maybe Farah will play soccer or decide to do ballet. Maybe it will turn out that Xavier really likes basketball, or wants to follow his old man onto the football field. However they decide to express themselves athletically, I know I am going into parenthood armed with the best information available to keep them healthy, and to give them the best opportunity to excel at the activities that make them happy. That's why writing this book is so important to me — all parents deserve this information. Because all kids deserve the best opportunity to excel.

2

THE ORGAN SYSTEMS

 "In order to understand how to keep your kid healthy, you need to have some basic knowledge about the core components of the growing body."

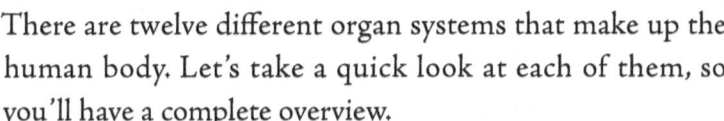

There are twelve different organ systems that make up the human body. Let's take a quick look at each of them, so you'll have a complete overview.

SKELETAL SYSTEM

The skeletal system is composed of all the bones that make up the rigid internal structure of our bodies. It serves many functions — giving our body a framework onto which everything else is suspended and supported being the most obvious. It also allows us to move, protects our internal organs like our heart, lungs, liver and brain, and houses the marrow, which forms the core of our bones and makes blood cells. The tendons and ligaments that hold muscles to bones or bones to bones are also a part of the skeletal system and are often the focus of attention when caring for an athlete.

MUSCULAR SYSTEM

There are three kinds of muscles: *skeletal*, a voluntary muscle, meaning that its motion is under our control, such as our bicep that contracts when we decide to lift our forearm and our quad that extends our lower leg when we want to walk from one place to another; *smooth*, an involuntary muscle, meaning that it works whether we tell it to or not, such as the muscles of our respiratory system that continue our breathing even when we aren't thinking specifically about breathing; and *cardiac*, another involuntary muscle group with properties of both skeletal and smooth muscle, that keeps our heart beating. The muscular system is controlled through the nervous system, and it works in concert with the skeletal system to allow us to move — walk and run and dance, jump and swim and carry a football over the goal line.

CIRCULATORY SYSTEM

Sometimes also called the cardiovascular system, the circulatory system transports such vital elements as blood, nutrients, oxygen, and hormones through our bodies. Humans have what is known as a *closed* circulatory system, meaning the blood itself doesn't normally leave the body's network of blood vessels, but the important things that blood carries, such as nutrients and oxygen, diffuse through the blood vessel walls and into the cells of the body's other systems that need the nourishment.

LYMPHATIC SYSTEM

The lymphatic system complements the circulatory system, but unlike that system it is not closed. Indeed, one of its primary functions is to act as a sort of alternative route for fluids, such as plasma (even though plasma is really a component of blood), of the circulatory system— for example, the circulatory system processes and filters over three-quarters of the blood in our bodies every day; it is the lymphatic system that picks up the slack. The lymphatic system is also a crucial part of our immune system, helping to filter our body's waste products and other debris, such as bacteria, and remove them from our bodies.

RESPIRATORY SYSTEM

Every time we inhale (thanks to those smooth muscles in our muscular system) we enrich the blood with oxygen (which the circulatory system then delivers to every cell in our body). The circulatory system also gathers up our body's waste, such as the gas carbon dioxide, a by-product of our body's functions, which we expel via our respiratory system every time we exhale. But the respiratory system— which consists of our mouth, nose, trachea, lungs, and diaphragm— not only takes in air and releases it, it also filters the air of foreign matter such as germs and pollution by way of cilia, very fine hairs coated with mucous that line our larynx, trachea, and bronchi.

IMMUNE SYSTEM

Our immune system, at least 70% of which is located in our gut wall, exists to protect us from disease. It is on alert to detect a stunning variety of pathogens— or infectious agents, such as germs, viruses, bacteria, fungi— and defend the body against them. A healthy, active immune system distinguishes these infectious agents from healthy tissue and responds by sending "fighter cells" to do combat with any invaders. Sometimes we can sense our immune systems at work — when we bump our knee and see swelling at the site of the injury, for example; swelling, redness, itching, and warmth can all be signs of those fighter cells in action. As you read this paragraph, you probably see words that you typically associate with inflammation — swelling, redness, itching, and so forth. This is one of those tricky places in medicine as inflammation and immune function are very closely related processes. We'll talk more specifically about inflammation versus immune function later in this book as it is crucially important in athletics of any sort of make sure both of these processes are well managed.

ENDOCRINE SYSTEM

The endocrine system's function is to secrete hormones and send hormonal signals to other parts of our bodies. Hormones are principally secreted by specialized parts of our bodies called glands. Think of the endocrine system as the body's gossip hotline, though the glandular system spreads its information even faster than the juiciest gossip could hope to travel. The hormones manufactured and secreted in the glands regulate both our body's development as we grow, and how it functions when we are adults. The pituitary gland, though just a pea-sized organism at the base of the brain, is also known as the body's "master gland" because of the number of hormones it produces (and therefore the number of the body's functions that it controls), and because the hormones it secretes tell other glands how to act. The thyroid gland, located in your neck, regulates your metabolism, or how fast your body can break down the nutrients in food to use them to fuel your activities, so its health can have an impact on your weight and fitness level. The pineal gland, located in your brain, produces, for example, melatonin, a hormone that determines how restfully you sleep by regulating your sleep-wake cycles, and this gland also helps to regulate sexual development.

INTEGUMENTARY SYSTEM

The Integumentary system is just a fancy name for our skin and other features of our bodies that make us waterproof, such as our hair and our finger- and toenails. This system also helps to hold our insides together and cushions us, protecting our internal organs and the deeper levels of our tissues from blows and abrasions.

REPRODUCTIVE SYSTEM

The reproductive system, or genital system, is composed of our sex organs. While a liver is a liver, and a brain is a brain, and skin is skin, this is the only system in our bodies where there is a difference of appearance and function between the boys and the girls.

URINARY SYSTEM

The purpose of this system, also called the renal system, is to eliminate waste from our bodies. The kidneys have a rich supply of blood vessels through which they filter our blood, sending clean blood back into our circulatory system and waste, in the form of urine, out of the body by way of *ureters*, to the *bladder*, where it makes its final exit through the *urethra*. Just to clarify a technicality you may be wondering about, the only difference between the male and the female urinary system is the *length* of the urethra.

THE DIGESTIVE SYSTEM

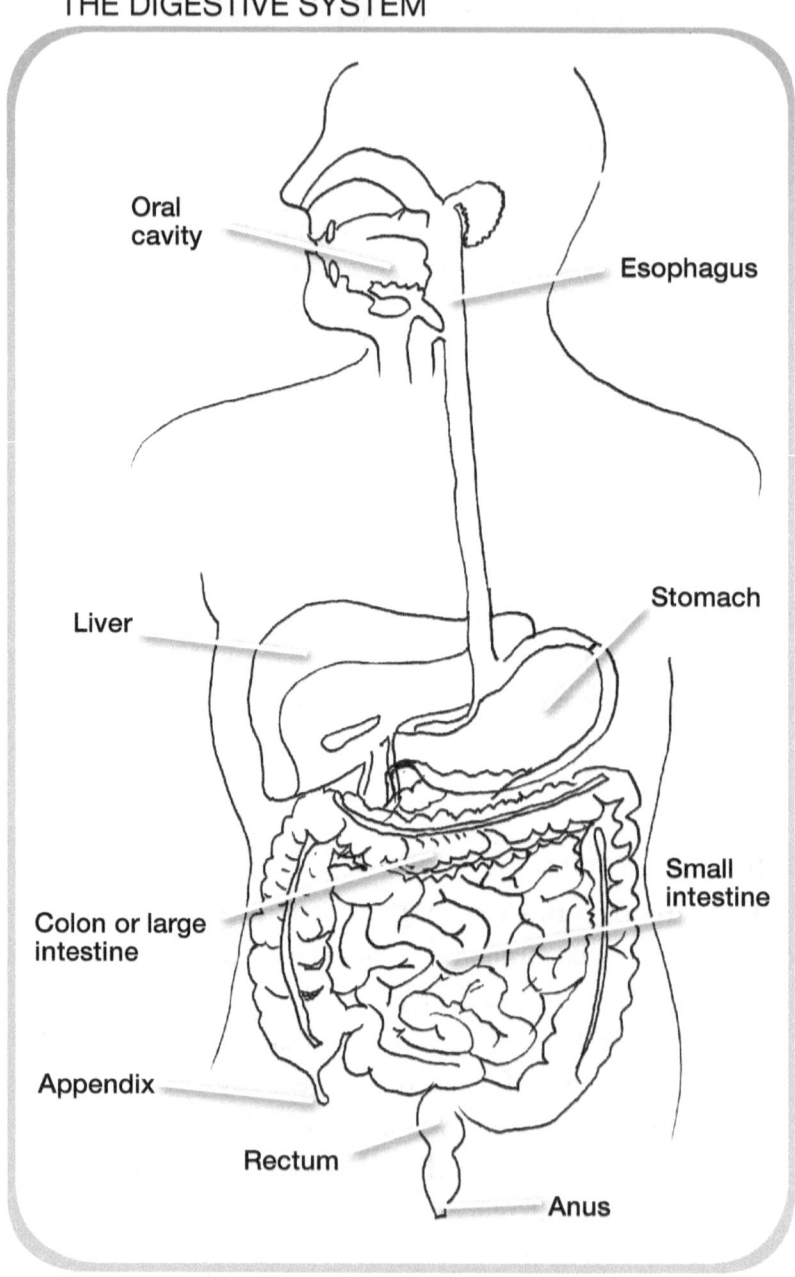

Oral cavity

Esophagus

Liver

Stomach

Colon or large intestine

Small intestine

Appendix

Rectum

Anus

DIGESTIVE SYSTEM

Our digestive systems break down food into ever smaller pieces, or particles, so our bodies can more easily use the food for fuel. The process of breaking down begins in the mouth where the food is mashed by the teeth and the action of the tongue and saliva begins the chemical deconstruction process. As food is transformed in the mouth from a bite to what we call a bolus, it is swallowed into the esophagus and moves further into the bowel, to the stomach. There, gastric juices continue the deconstruction, continuing to turn chicken, for example, to amino acids, fats, minerals, and some vitamins. As the digestive process continues, rhythmic contraction of muscles along the wall of the stomach move the nutrients to the small intestine where they are absorbed into the bloodstream and taken by way of the circulatory system to the hungry cells in our body. The liver, and the bile made within it, the spleen, the gallbladder, and the pancreas, which is actually a gland — you see how our human bodies overlap and interweave together, complex but so elegant — all then do their part to do things like break down carbohydrates and proteins, emulsify fat, or regulate the glucose (sugar) in our blood. Digested food gathers in our large intestine, also known as our colon, moves relatively slowly — from twelve to up to fifty hours — toward the exit, the anus. Along the way water is gradually removed over time, and it then leaves our bodies as poop. The quality of our poop is a subject we're going to take up at length later in this book because the regularity of when we poop, and the poop's color, consistency, size, shape, contents, and odor are all wonderful if sorely neglected indicators of our general health. We just don't talk enough about poop! But rest assured, we're going to correct that in the upcoming pages.

How Much Should Your Kid Weigh?

One of my patients, a fourteen-year-old tennis player named Amy, came in with her mom for her annual well-child visit—and because Mom had called before the appointment to give me a head's up, I anticipated Amy's concern, though for a lot of kids, especially girls, the concern is, unfortunately, not uncommon. "I weigh too much," Amy told me.

But Amy did not weigh too much. Not at all. She was in the 59th BMI percentile, which indicated a healthy weight, and it was my job to explain to her what BMI, or Body Mass Index, was, and how it was calculated, and why she was at a weight that was really pretty much perfect.

BMI is a tool doctors and other health professionals use to screen our patients for potential health problems based on *the amount of body fat they carry*. BMI is calculated from a person's weight as well as their height, their sex, and their age, and it is calculated a little differently for children and teens than it is for adults. The Centers for Disease Control and Prevention has a handy, online child and teen BMI calculator[1] that you can use to find out the percentile into which your child, aged two to nineteen, fits. Children who fall below the 5th percentile are considered underweight, and those who fall above the 85th percentile are considered overweight. Children who exceed the 95th percentile are considered obese.

_____

1 http://nccd.cdc.gov/dnpabmi/Calculator.aspx.

NERVOUS SYSTEM

You've likely noticed as you've read along how interconnected all the various body systems are. Though they each perform their own distinct functions in the body, they all have to work together in harmony. The nervous system is one of the ways that the various systems of the body are

I could easily go into my rant about how the fact that the farming methods of big agriculture have stripped our foods—apples and spinach and peaches and lettuce and such—of the amount of nutrition they contained just a generation ago. About how junk food, and junk-food advertisers, are poisoning our children and depriving them of the nutrition they need to excel both physically and mentally. About how both of these factors contribute to the epidemic of childhood obesity we're experiencing today in this country—and about how the portrayal of young women in mass-media advertising contributes to the corollary problem of rampant teenage and young-adult eating disorders. But that could be a book unto itself.

Suffice it here to say that just because a child falls within a healthy BMI percentile does not mean that she isn't suffering from an eating disorder. If you suspect your child has an eating disorder, there are resources you can access to help you talk with her in a calm and positive way, as well as find out what steps to take to facilitate a constructive intervention.[2]

Here, however, is the real kicker for our young athletes: because muscle weighs more than fat, our active girls as well as our boys can expect their BMI to be slightly higher than average. If your child is worried about his or her weight, check her BMI first—explain to her how it works, and enlist your doctor's help, if necessary, to guide her toward achieving a healthy BMI percentile.

---

2 http://www.nationaleatingdisorders.org/find-help-support.

connected together. It allows them to talk to each other and helps to coordinate their functions. The brain and the spinal cord—known as your central nervous system (CNS)—along with your sensory organs (such as your eyes, ear, and tongue) and all the nerves that connect them, make up the nervous system.

SOME OF OUR organs are referred to as "vital" organs. These include organs such as the heart and brains and lungs, which are critical to life — to living. That is, it is possible to live without, say, our spleen, or our ovaries, but we cannot stay alive without a functioning heart. And to function at our highest physical potential, we have to take care of every part of every single one of these systems.

The organ systems are all present and most are fully functional in our bodies at birth, but they continue to grow in size and heaviness as we grow to adulthood. Think of this: while it is impossible to actually count the number of cells in a human body, and even if you could you couldn't say for sure that every human being contained the exact same number of cells because you'd have to account for things like the height and weight of each particular human being — but let's just say that Eugene, who towers over me at 6'4" contains a whole lot more cells than I do simply because he is so much taller than I am. But *on average*, the body of a fully-grown person is made up of between fifty and seventy *trillion* cells. In contrast, a newborn's body is made up, on average, of about only two trillion cells. That's a minimum of forty-eight trillion cells each newborn body will have to manufacture in the course of growing up — think of the pounds of food and the tons of oxygen the newborn will require to have the energy necessary to perform the heroic task of growing up!

In utero and throughout her infancy, childhood, and adolescence, her nervous system, immune system, respiratory system, and reproductive organs will undergo major changes. For example, the alveoli, or the air sacs in her lungs, which is the place where oxygen from the air she breathes enters her blood, will continue to increase in number and won't stop increasing until some time in late adolescence.

The growth of the skeletal system and the nervous system are so extensive that we've devoted complete sections just to them, which you'll see in the following pages.

 " My two-year old daughter needs more food than I do…"

Because a kid's organ systems are so immature, it takes a whole lot more resources to sustain them than it does to sustain the organ systems of an adult. Pound for pound, children breathe more air, drink more water, and consume more food than adults — between the ages of one and five years, kids eat three to four times more per pound of body weight than the average adult![1]

But here's the thing that really alarms Nureya and me: the higher rate of intake means that kids can potentially receive even higher doses of environmental toxins than adults. If I eat an apple that's been grown with the use of petrochemical fertilizers or pesticides, I get a dose — per pound of my body weight — of those petrochemicals in every mouthful. My three-year-old, Farah, however, with every bite she takes, gets a dose so much higher than I do. This is why it is so critical that kids get as much locally grown and organic produce and other foods as possible. I know Julie is going to cover the science of that in more detail in an upcoming section of this book, but I don't want to pass up an opportunity to say it again.

1 http://www.nrdc.org/health/kids/ocar/chap2.asp

3

THE SKELETON AND MUSCLES

 *"*Changing from Gumby to G.I. Joe—going from that level of malleability to a hard plastic—that's actually not a bad way to think of growing bones…*"*

When a baby is born, its skeleton is composed of three hundred parts, and many of these parts are made of cartilage, a soft but tough, elastic tissue of the sort we grown-ups find in our ears and nose. As the baby grows, the cartilage becomes bone through a process called *ossification*, during which cartilage cells are replaced by bone cells. Additionally, its bones fuse so that, by the time that baby becomes an adult, most of the cartilage has become solid bone and its adult skeleton is composed of only the requisite two hundred and six parts.

Think about that. A child starts out with three hundred different skeletal parts and, over the years, those parts grow and fuse so that the number is reduced by almost 33%. That's an enormous amount of organic merging going on in the small body, and all that merging helps to explain what we so often refer to as our child's "awkward stage." Your child may grow a quarter inch over the course of one night's sleep, and her legs may then be an eighth of an inch longer in the morning, but when she wakes up her brain doesn't know yet that she's grown. Her brain needs time to adjust to the new length of her limbs, and to learn how to coordinate the way that she uses them. Don't miss the irony here: our kids are trying to be body conscious and aware at a time when their bodies sometimes change more rapidly than they can assimilate. The result sometimes impacts their coordination, their confidence, and their self-esteem.

Sometimes, in up to about 40% of our kids, growing can actually be painful. We refer to this phenomenon, commonly, as "growing pains." Generally, such pains — often described by youngsters as *throbbing*— occur during two specific periods in childhood: in early childhood, between ages three and five, and then again later, at between eight and twelve, although teenagers will often complain of similar, mysterious pains.

I say "mysterious" because there is no peer-reviewed evidence that suggests the act of growing bones is actually painful. Some doctors believe that the cause of the throbbing is the activity the kids themselves participate in, and if a child who is prone to such aches has an especially active day, running and jumping and such, then you can expect complaints at the end of the day. It has also been suggested that the pain is a result of the skin of the bone, the periosteum, stretching tightly as the bone it covers grows very rapidly.

Whatever the cause, such pains can be a sign that the child's body needs even more additional nutritional assistance to do its job of growing to become an adult body. Specifically, it may be crying out for more calcium, magnesium, and/or Vitamin D. Unfortunately, growing pains occur at just the stages in life when our kids tend to turn into "picky eaters" — or, in the case of teenagers, "independent eaters" who prefer fries and sodas and other fast "food" with their peers to well-balanced meals around the family table. Getting them to eat the servings of spinach, kale, and bok choy that could more organically solve the problem can be a challenge, and this is where good-quality vitamin and mineral supplements can fill the void.

Interestingly, the medical world is beginning to understand that most of us really need more magnesium, and Vitamin D3, and iodine, and fatty acids, and — fill in the blank here — than we thought our bodies needed, something we'll cover in more detail a little later on. The take-away I want to impress upon you at this point is that most of us are woefully undernourished if we are doing anything except eating purely organic, nutrient-dense foods. This is especially true of our children, who are trying to grow gazillions of new cells while simultaneously exercising, which requires additional energy and micronutrients on a regular basis. When we talk more about diet and nutrition, we'll give you some useful guidelines you can use as you talk with your child about healthy eating and/or determine what supplements could be helpful to him.

GROWING PAINS CAN occur in the child's joints — especially knees, hand, and feet — and in her muscles, often in the calves, behind the knees, the quads or the front of her thighs or, classically, on the shins, and these pains aren't consistent, meaning they come and go from day to day, or week to week. They can be most intense in the late afternoons and early evenings, though with some children the pain happens overnight and is so powerful it will wake him up. What do you do when your child wakes up crying from this seemingly phantom pain? There are several things you can do to help. Try having your child do a few simple stretching exercises — sitting on the floor with the legs in a 'V' position and bending gently over each leg, or flexing the toes up toward the knees. Massaging the area that hurts can also be effective, as can a warm Epsom salts bath or a heating pad placed over the part of the body that aches. Some children feel more relief with a cool towel placed over the sore area — everyone is different. As a last resort, you might want to give her ibuprofen as an over-the-counter pain reliever. I avoid recommending acetaminophen as it reduces glutathione synthesis, something that our bodies really need and have a hard time supplying adequately. Remember that no pain reliever should be used day in and day out, including both ibuprofen and acetaminophen, and that you never want to give a child under twelve years of age aspirin because it has been associated with Reye's syndrome.[1]

One thing to keep at the forefront of your mind, especially when it is two AM and you're drawing yet another bath for your crying kid in the middle of the night: growing pains are legit. Yes, your child will seem as if he is completely cured of any complaint by the time the sun rises, but I assure you he has not faked the pain. The pain is real and he needs your reassurance and support while he's going through it.

Sometimes a child experiences pain to such an extent that it can really rattle us parents. When should you consider taking your child to your doctor?

To doctors, growing pains are a diagnosis of exclusion. That means, depending on the symptoms your child presents with, your doctor will want to rule out other conditions before settling on the growing-pain diagnosis. A

---

1 http://www.ncbi.nlm.nih.gov/pubmedhealth/PMH0002532/

thorough medical history as well as a physical exam, sometimes including blood tests, X-rays, or other medical tests,
will help your doctor to make the diagnosis. But be sure
that you do call your doctor if your child has any of these
symptoms:

- Touch worsens the pain, or your child responds
  negatively to touch; children with growing pains
  generally want to be held, or cuddled.
- The pain is persistent, occurs or continues in the
  morning, or is accompanied by swelling, redness, or
  unusual rashes in the painful area.
- The pain is accompanied by fever.
- Your child is limping.
- You can track the pain back to a specific injury.
- Your child exhibits a loss of appetite, weakness, is
  especially tired, or demonstrates another behavior
  that isn't normal or characteristic of him.

GROWTH PLATES

A child's bones grow by virtue of *growth plates*, which are
also called epiphyseal plates, located at each end of each
bone. The growth plate is, simply, an area of tissue composed of cells whose *sole purpose* is to create longer bones.
The growth plates are thought to close at late adolescence,
normally at between twelve and fourteen for girls, and sixteen to eighteen for boys. Boys' plates close more slowly
than girls', so they are vulnerable to injury for a longer
period of time. Indeed, they are quite possibly still growing
even when the child is in college. For all children, boys as
well as girls, the growth plates are the weakest points in the
growing skeleton, and therefore most vulnerable to injury.

GROWTH PLATES, FRONT OF ARM

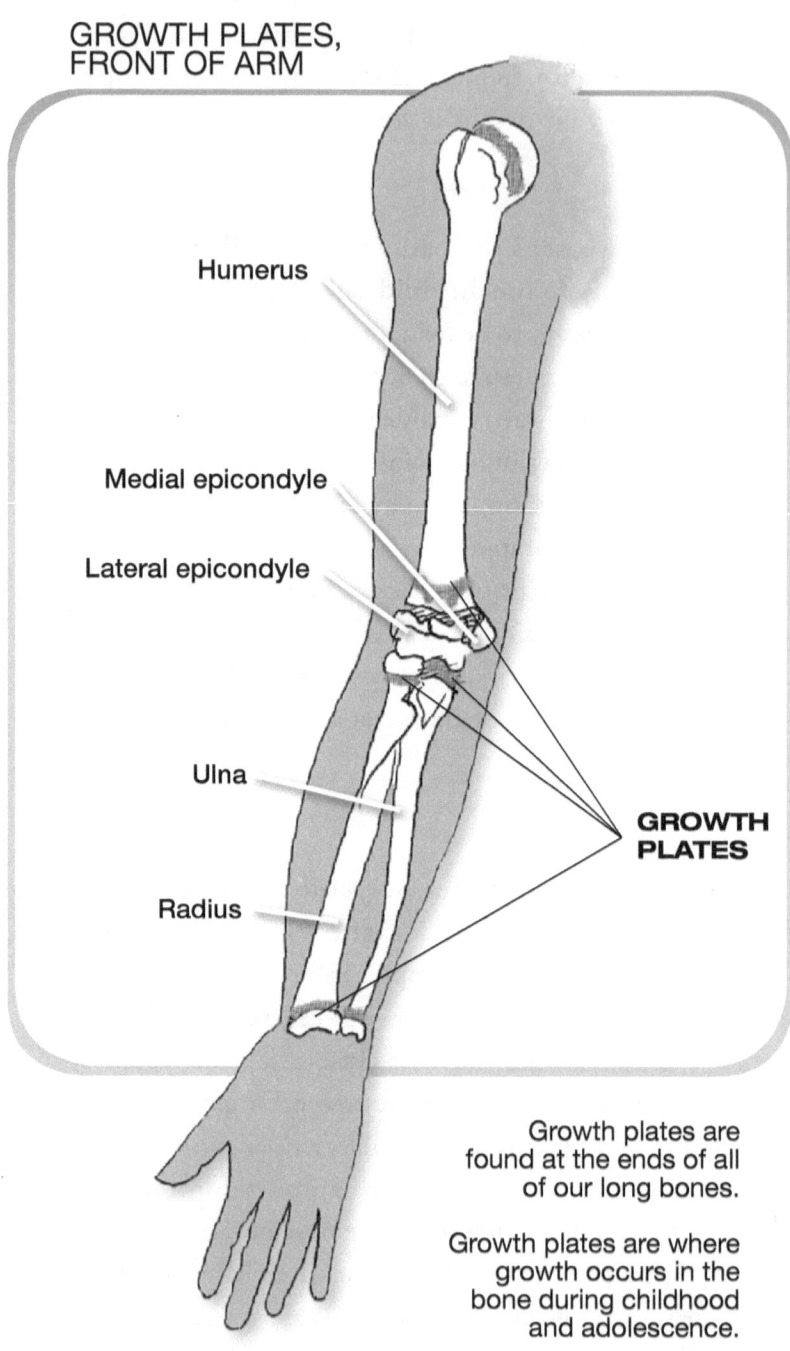

Humerus

Medial epicondyle

Lateral epicondyle

Ulna

Radius

GROWTH PLATES

Growth plates are found at the ends of all of our long bones.

Growth plates are where growth occurs in the bone during childhood and adolescence.

A full third of growth-plate injuries occur when kids are playing competitive sports, and an additional 20% occur as the result of other recreational activities such as sledding and biking. These injuries can be caused as the result of a fall, a blow, and they can also result from overuse of the joint and associated muscles, for example pitching in a baseball game. This is the very reason, in fact, that Little League International has been such an advocate of pitch counts, to protect young and growing arms.

Think of a young joint — shoulder, elbow, hip, knee — as if it is a pot being thrown on a wheel. The potter is molding it, shaping it, trying to turn it into the beautiful, functional object — let's say a water pitcher — it can become. But it isn't finished yet, and you wouldn't cut it off the wheel and try to use it when only its bottom half was complete, it wasn't yet dry, and didn't yet have a spout. When you try to make a growing kid perform as if she is a grown, professional athlete, this is when injuries — that could be permanent — can happen. The baseball pitcher and the water pitcher both need a chance to finish growing and take the shape of what they are going to become before we expect them to function optimally and at their full capacity.

The ends of bones, where a child's growth plates are located, are also the place where either tendons attach the bone to muscle, or where ligaments attach that bone to another bone. No matter how strong you are, this is the weakest part of the musculoskeletal structure: the place where the muscle cells come together with tendon to join to the bone. This is generally where a muscle will tear or rip and result in injury, even for an adult whose growth plates have long since matured and closed. For a youngster, the vulnerability is even more significant because the growth plate, near to where the tendon or ligament is attached, is still open and is more easily disrupted.

"How long can you keep growing?"

I was in my mid-twenties, and a professional football player, and I thought of myself as fully-grown. After working with Julie, changing the way I ate and taking advantage of other therapies Julie and I will talk about later in this book, *I grew an additional quarter inch*. The human body is miraculous in its potential. That's why it's so important to take such good care of the body you have — you only get one, and it has to last you your whole life long, and, if you're like me, you want it to work and feel its best every single day.

4

THE NERVOUS SYSTEM AND
THE YOUNG BRAIN

 " Kids are not
little adults. *"*

The human nervous system — which includes, of course, the brain — is a structure more elegant and complex than most of us can possibly imagine. It's worth taking a few moments to give you an overview of this amazing biological arrangement.

That lump of grayish, rather play-doh-ish organic material that sits inside our skulls is a mini-universe. It is the command center of our *central nervous system* — which consists of our brain and our spinal cord — made up of approximately one hundred billion specialized cells, called neurons. We very often think of the brain as this isolated computer stuck on top of our bodies, running it from a distance. But to quote my friend Martha Herbert, MD, PhD, *"Folks, the brain is wet, and it is connected to the body."*

Neurons are the highly specialized cells of our nervous system. They line up, sort of head to tail, and create a superhighway they use as the pathway by which our body "talks" to itself.

A neuron is a pretty funny looking cell. It has a star-shaped cell body with little "tree branches", called dendrites,

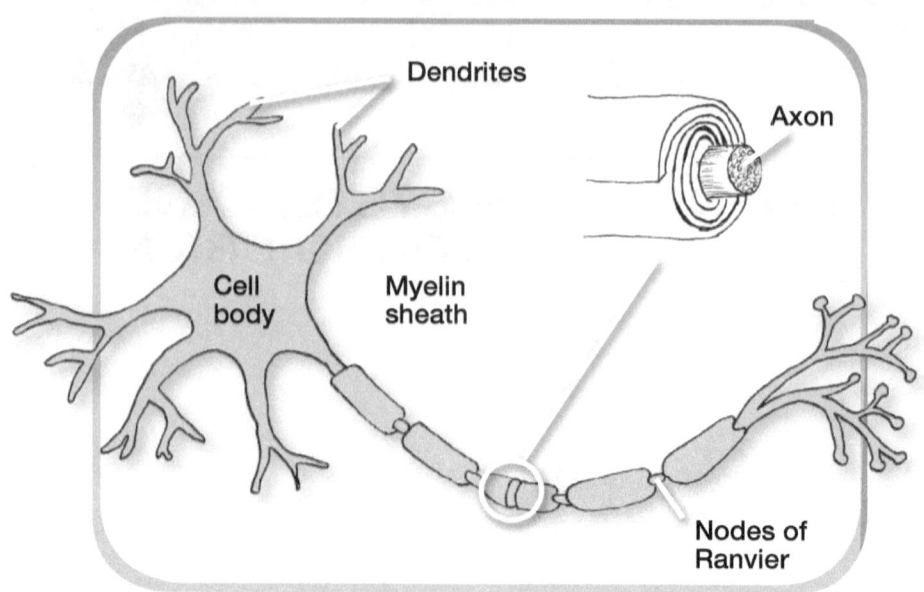

Dendrites

Axon

Cell body

Myelin sheath

Nodes of Ranvier

protruding from each tip. Each neuron has one star tip that is much longer than the others. This long tip is called the axon and it ends in more little dendrites. Some axons are just long and smooth. Other axons are wrapped up in a coating called myelin and those axons look like a long string of sausage links. The dendrites at the end of the axon of one cell snuggle up close to the dendrites of the next cell, leaving an infinitesimal space between the two neurons called the synapse. Our body sends messages from one cell to the next along a superhighway that is thousands of neurons long, sort of a neuronal "whispering down the lane", but a lot more precise.

Now that we've got the anatomy of the cell and its neural pathway built, we can learn the amazing *way* that the messages get sent down the neuronal superhighway. This is critically important to understand in order to make sense of head injury and what happens to neural pathways when they are injured.

Messages travel along the neuron as electrical impulses. They can make their way down the smooth axon relatively slowly, or they can leap frog much more quickly from one myelinated sausage link to the next. Here's the fascinating part: to get the message from one neuron to the next, the electrical signal traveling down the axon must be converted to a chemical messages in the synapse between the cells.

These chemical messengers are called *neurotransmitters*. Neurotransmitters are, simply put, special messenger chemicals that our body manufactures in order to communicate with its various parts. You may be familiar with some of them — amino acids, such as glutamate (which is what makes our synapses fire), and monoamines, like serotonin and dopamine (which have dozens of functions in the body but are best known as part of our systems of pleasure regulation and cognitive function). It is worth saying here that hormones, like estrogen and testosterone, are produced in our glands and, though they are not classified as neurotransmitters, also play the part of messengers. A big difference between neurotransmitters and hormones is that, while neurotransmitters are confined to traveling along existing nerve pathways, hormones can access every part of the body's circulatory system, though they do so at a relatively slower speed — signals from neurons clock in at milliseconds, and signals from hormones can take anywhere from a second to hours to be fully received.

The path the message takes, from one specific cell to another, is called a *neural network*. Neural networks have everything to do with the way the brain learns — for everyone, not just our kids. When we are first exposed to a new piece of information — from "two plus two equals four" to "If I leave my dirty socks in the middle of the living room floor my mom gets mad." — this information creates an electrical pathway in our brain. If we hear the information repeated often enough — or *study* the information, as we do when we're in school — the electrical pathway in our brain grows stronger, and even permanent. This explains why rote learning can work well for learning things like multiplication tables and what we call "muscle memory", as well as why you have to tell your kid to pick up his dirty socks fifty times before he actually remembers to do it.

Now, these specialized brain cells — neurons — are divided into even more specialized groups. The walk you take from the refrigerator to the sink while you're making your lunch, your ability to clap to show appreciation at a concert, your decision to wrap your hand around a football and toss it to another player — these messages are all sent to muscles by *motor neurons* that control our voluntary movements. The way you experience the color of the football, the sound of the crowd cheering at the game, and the taste of the peanuts you buy from the stadium vendor — that is, a thing or event you experience by way of your senses — is controlled by your *sensory neurons*. Your involuntary responses — the way your eyes dilate to adjust to a lighted football field at night or the way your body digests the peanuts — is controlled by other parts of the nervous system that are, generally, grouped together as the *autonomic nervous system*. Together, all of these nerves and their terms comprise *the peripheral nervous system*. The peripheral nervous system is the term we use for just about everything that is the nervous system outside of the brain itself. The peripheral nervous system — using those superhighway neural pathways, sending electrical-chemical-electrical-chemical messages — connects your brain to every other part of your body — your skeletal muscles and your internal organs, for example.

So, THESE ARE the components of our nervous system—but that system isn't fully functional when we are born. Let me give you an example we can all relate to.

We are familiar with the idea that our bones lengthen and our muscles strengthen as we grow during our first year so we can learn to walk. Similarly, the nervous system has to mature before we're able to take our first steps. This "tandem" development ensures that the body, growing in ways that will allow it to perform more and more complicated actions physically, keeps pace with the brain, that grows in ways that allow it to both better coordinate the body's actions *and* begin to understand why and how it is taking those actions.

Let's talk more specifically about the brain. It functions at birth, of course, but not in the way that it will when we're adults. And just when is it that, that our brains become "adult brains"? When does the brain stop growing? How old are we when we're officially considered adult and the brain is finished developing?

Well, I want to make a distinction at this point between the growth phase of the brain from infancy to adulthood, and the *plasticity* of the brain, which continues for our whole lives. Plasticity is, simply put, the capability to change and adapt. Continuing to read and to learn, to be curious about and participate both physically and mentally in the world around us "exercises" the brain, keeping the neural pathways we already have in tip-top shape and even forging new ones. This is why, if the brain is injured—say, because of a concussion or a stroke—it has the ability to recover. Can the brain fully recover from each and every injury? That depends on the extent of the injury, the speed and efficacy of the rehabilitative therapy we receive, and how hard we ourselves are able and willing to work to restore its function. But, at the bottom line, yes, our brains are capable of repairing damaged neural pathways and of creating new, alternative pathways when the old ones have been damaged beyond repair. Our brains retain this ability for our whole lives.

It is worth noting here that the understanding that nerves and brains can heal is relatively new. I remember learning in medical school and residency that nerves didn't come back once they were damaged and/or dead, that neurons grew too slowly to ever rebuild a neural superhighway once it was destroyed, and that there wasn't a whole lot you could do for a nerve once it was injured. It's a pretty exciting time in my functional medicine world now, because a mere two decades later, our understanding is changing dramatically, giving hope where there really wasn't any, and, honestly, making a lot of docs who were trained a long time ago very uncomfortable. When I have discussions about neurological *stuff* with older doctors who were trained "back in the day," they sometimes remind me of the conversations I used to have with my dad about music. He shared his love of Elvis with me, and we listened to *Hound Dog*, *Jailhouse Rock*, and *Love Me Tender* regularly. When Bruce Springsteen and Michael Jackson came on the scene, however, my father insisted that what they were doing wasn't music — because he couldn't understand the lyrics I was singing at the top of my lungs, and there wasn't harmony — at least harmony with which he was familiar — woven into the melody.

Getting back to the changeable, adaptable nervous system, and our changing, adapting understanding of it, let's consider actual growth — the actual increase in the numbers of neurons in a body. In terms of the brain's growth from infancy to full maturity, there is a finite end point, though what that end point is has, itself, been subject to revision as technology allows us to know ever more about how the brain really works.

For centuries it was the conventional wisdom that the "age of reason", or the age at which a child begins to assume "moral responsibility" — the age at which the brain was fully functional — was seven. *Seven years old.* I don't know about you but, much as I adore children who are seven years old, I would not assume their responsibility for understanding or making considered moral judgments. Although seven-year-olds do often ask the most amazing questions about religion and politics, this is exactly why they are not allowed to sign contracts or hold elective office. During my years in medical school — the 1980s — it was the conventional wisdom that the brain reached its maturity in the teenage years. That was a leap forward over the old way of thinking about the age of intellectual and emotional maturity, but I ask every adult reading this book if they'd like to be held responsible for some of the decisions they made at eighteen. Or twenty.

These days, thanks to various technologies that allow us to more accurately observe living brain tissue, even while it is in the *process* of thinking, we understand that the brain doesn't come into its own until we're somewhere in our mid-twenties.

How do we know this? What have we learned about the brain's development that allows us to understand this?

One of the phenomena of brain development that scientists have been able to observe is the process of *myelination.* *Myelin,* which we already touched upon a few pages ago, is a protein that functions as a nerve cell's "electrical insulation". It forms a sheath around the axons of our neurons and this aids — really *speeds* — the transmission of the electrical messages down the axon so the cells can talk to each other, as well as to different areas of the brain, accurately and rapidly. Imagine the difference between walking, one foot in front of the other, down a path, versus being able to jump, leap-frogging down the same path. Sending a message down a myelinated neuron goes an awful lot faster than sending that message down an unmyelinated neuron. Myelination is the process of developing these protective sheaths — and that process isn't complete for humans until we are in our *mid-twenties*. Disrupting this process of myelination — or damaging the myelin sheath that already exists — is part of what happens to the brain during a head injury. We are learning that *remyelinating* might be something that the human brain can actually do; spontaneous remyelination has been observed to occur in patients with multiple sclerosis lesions.[1] The extent to which this does or can occur in the general population is yet unknown, but research continues and, if it turns out to be the case that the brain can heal in this way, it would change everything in terms of managing chronic neurologic issues and diseases.

The on-going construction zone that is a kid's brain, however, can't be explained only by the process of myelination. It isn't only the circuitry of the brain that isn't quite complete. As kids grow up they are also adding neural networks at a rapid pace, as well as pruning them — this latter is especially mysterious, though scientists speculate that the brain is deciding which neural networks to keep based on how frequently they're used. Additionally, the way the different parts of the brain are used — that is, for example, the parts of the brain that are used to solve a problem or resolve a social situation — are very different for young people than they are for those of us whose brains are fully formed.

---

1 http://brain.oxfordjournals.org/content/129/12/3165.

Then, to complicate matters further, as they hit their teens, our kids' brain functions are also impacted by an influx of hormones. Most of us, when we think of teenagers and hormones, think immediately about sex-related growth and behaviors. But estrogen and testosterone have roles that extend far beyond sex-related development, and they are not by a long shot the only hormones running newly rampant in the adolescent body. Broad and enormous hormonal changes take place in adolescence, most notably affecting the hormones that impact general social behavior as well as how the child deals with stress.

One area where the adolescent brain has it all over the fully-formed adult brain is learning — the teenage brain is primed to learn and will never again in its life be so receptive to processing new information. But other than this real advantage, the teen's and even young adult's ability to make good decisions, control her impulses, and regulate her emotional reactions are not yet wholly developed because the parts of her brain that would allow her to do these things are not yet wholly developed. Take, for example, the part of the brain known as the *prefrontal cortex*. This is the part of the brain that is command central, where we do our highest thinking, problem-solving, reasoning, and complex decision-making. It is another part of the brain that isn't fully formed until we are in the middle of our twenties. That's why teenagers often make impulsive and seemingly irresponsible decisions that drive their parents crazy. They do things that we think, in fact, are just plain stupid, because that's what they're *equipped* to do at that age — and why we, as parents, are so often called upon to impose a more informed judgment on their decisions. I can't say it often enough: **kids are not little adults.** If you put a fourteen year old in a situation and ask him to make the same sort of call you'd expect from someone who is thirty — well, don't be surprised if that doesn't work out very well.

Each time period of our child's life has a different name — infant, toddler, early childhood, tweens, teens. These different names correspond, more or less roughly depending on the development of the individual child, to the level at which their brains have developed. We don't expect an infant to know how to spell, but we do expect someone in early childhood to start learning the skill; we don't expect a toddler to be able to train as a downhill skier, but we would put a tween on skis and send her into a beginner class.

Just as we can't expect our kids to make good decisions or have excellent, adult-level judgment as children, or tweens, or teens, we can't expect their physical bodies or brains to handle the same sorts of stresses that an adult body will be able to deal with efficiently. Certainly we can't expect their bodies to perform at the same level as we expect our professional athletes to perform.

" Let's pretend your brain is a rubber ducky... *"*

I wear a helmet every day when I go to work. That's the time-honored way we football players try to protect our heads from injury — at least it has been for about a hundred and twenty years, since some football player, there's debate about exactly who, made a helmet out of leather to protect his ears. It was hot inside leather helmets, and they didn't offer a whole lot of protection, but that's what football players wore up until the 1950s. That's when you started to see innovations like plastic shells and padding, visors and even headsets on the field.

Lately you hear a lot about H. I. T. (head impact telemetry), which is a software system that involves putting sensors inside helmets so that, when a player gets hit, the impact can be measured in real time. H. I. T. will give doctors and scientists more of the sorts of information they need to understand how head injuries, including concussions, happen. And it's probably going to be really helpful in having accurate information about head injuries that happen in the course of play, because players at all levels underreport them. *But H. I. T. does nothing new to actually protect the wearer's head.*

That's because helmets — any helmets — don't really protect a player from potential head injuries. Physiologically, it is just not possible to adequately protect the brain by encasing the skull around it in any sort of covering. The brain sits in the skull in a pool of fluid — *cerebrospinal fluid*—that has a few different functions, but the one we're talking about here is that it acts as a buffer between the brain and the bone of the skull. To give you a clear picture of what this physiological arrangement means for an athlete, let's pretend your brain is a rubber ducky. Put that rubber ducky in the big drink cooler you use for tailgating and fill that cooler up with water. Then wrap that tub up as tightly as you can — wrap plastic around it and duct tape it and strap it around with bungee cords. Then shake that cooler up hard. No matter how protectively you wrap up the cooler, the rubber toy inside it is still going to career all over the place when you shake up the cooler, hitting the sides of the cooler over and over again.

That's what happens to your brain when you hit your head — or your head gets hit. One hit can cause a concussion, and *just that one concussion causes some level of damage.* But the cumulative effect — hit after hit, concussion after concussion — can often be much worse. That's because every time your brain bounces off your skull it causes *neuronal sheer* in which the neurons, and the pathways they've formed, are broken. Neuronal sheer is not hard to visualize. Just imagine putting a few rubber bands around a handful of uncooked spaghetti. Stand the spaghetti on end, then smack it really hard with a baseball bat. The spaghetti that breaks? Those are the neurons that experienced neuronal sheer. When neurons get broken it's like breaking our connection with what we know. Literally, the pathways that store our knowledge, our memories, and our understanding of the world around us — colors and aromas, places and dates and people, which can include even ourselves — are broken.

It's almost a given when you play football that you're going to get hit in the head. But in every sport there's a risk of concussion. That's why, both as an athlete and as a parent, I need to know everything I can about how I can keep my kids safe, and how I can help them to heal when they do take a hit.

 "Please tell me more…"

By now you should be in at least a little bit of awe of your neurons, and, if you're not, let me lay it out for you in very plain terms: every involuntary breath you take or morsel of food you digest, every voluntary move you make from smiling to running a marathon, is dictated by the billions of cells that make up your nervous system. And *how well you do all these things is dictated by the health of all the trillions of cells that make up the* whole *human body.*

How do we keep all the cells in our body healthy? That's Part Two. Keep reading.

II.

PREVENTING, RECOGNIZING, AND HEALING SPORTS INJURIES

5

FUNCTIONAL MEDICINE

 *"*More than half of our children's sports injuries are preventable—so what do we do to prevent them?*"*

I feel a great sense of urgency as I write this book, and that sense grows more intense with every news story I read about another high school or college athlete who died too young. Jeron Lewis, who collapsed on the court during the second half of Division II Southern Indiana's win over Kentucky Wesleyan in January 2010.[1] Wes Leonard, sixteen, of Fenville, Michigan, who died in 2011 while playing basketball.[2] Former Missouri State linebacker Michael Keck, who passed away in 2013.[3] Fourteen-year-old William Shogran, who died of heat stroke during football practice in August of 2014 in a town called Starke in my home state of Florida.[4] The three high school football players who died in the same week in October 2014 — Isaiah Langston,

---

1 http://espn.go.com/mens-college-basketball/story/_/id/8313100/when-hearts-young-athletes-fail-college-basketball.

2 http://www.cnn.com/2011/HEALTH/03/11/teen.heart.deaths/index.html.

3 http://www.si.com/college-football/2014/08/26/missouri-state-michael-keck-brain-trauma-cte.

4 http://www.palmbeachpost.com/ap/ap/florida/high-school-football-player-died-of-heat-stroke/nhyyb/#__federated=1.

seventeen, of North Carolina; Demario Harris, seventeen, of Alabama; Tom Cutinella, sixteen, of New York.[1]

Among the nation's estimated thirty-five million young athletes, an average of twelve of them will die each year due to sports-related injuries — these are the most heartrending cases. According to a study by the Centers for Disease Control (CDC) conducted in 2005-2006, high school athletes alone account for approximately two million injuries, half a million doctor visits, and thirty thousand hospitalizations annually.[2] Remember, that's high school only — three and a half million youth athletes receive medical treatment for sports injuries[3] and 12,500 college athletes are reported injured[4] every year.

Ready for a few more sobering statistics? *Overuse* is the cause of nearly half of all sports injuries among middle and high school students; a full 21% of all traumatic brain injuries among US children occur during participation in sports activities; and, according to the CDC, *more than half of all our children's sports injuries are preventable.*[5]

Let me repeat that: **more than half of all of our children's sports injuries are preventable.**

If we can keep over half of our kids from being injured while playing the sports they love — and that are so good for them to play — *why aren't we doing it?* From their earliest years, our children's safety is our top priorty. We load our kids into specially designed infant and toddler car seats, put up baby gates to prevent them from falling down the stairs when they're learning to walk, hold their chubby little hands and teach them to look both ways when crossing the

1   http://mashable.com/2014/10/03/high-school-football-player-deaths/.

2   http://www.cdc.gov/mmwr/preview/mmwrhtml/mm5538a1.htm.

3   http://www.stopsportsinjuries.org/media/statistics.aspx.

4   http://www.livestrong.com/article/513231-frequency-of-injury-among-college-athletes/.

5   http://www.stopsportsinjuries.org/media/statistics.aspx.

street. But from inadequate athlete screenings to lax safety precautions on the practice field, from failures to warm up and stretch properly to putting insufficient limits on their practice time, we — parents, coaches, athletic directors, schools and community youth sports organizations — are letting our kids down when it comes to making sure they participate in athletics in the most healthy and positive possible ways.

This failure, as I hope I've made clear in the previous sentence, is not the fault of parents — or, not parents alone. We live in a sports-obsessed culture — and I don't mean that statement as a negative. I myself am sports-obsessed, especially come football season — and I remind you that I allowed my own son to take the field. But when sports prowess becomes the primary lens through which we view our children — and/or when we forget that our children *are* children, and their bodies are not yet able to bear the stresses that adult bodies can handle — that's when we enter dangerous territory.

But before we talk about illness and injury, we should talk a little more about health. We use this important word — health — so carelessly, without really understanding fully what it means. In a nutshell, health is our natural state, at least until it is interrupted by illness or injury. And here's the kicker: the healthier we are to start with — the better we maintain our bodies — the less likely disease will find its way to us, and the fewer injuries we will suffer. The most fundamental way to understand health — our health and the health of our children — is through the lens of *functional medicine*.

"Before I met Julie, I knew zero about functional medicine."

Really. *Zero.*

But when I found out what it was, I couldn't get enough. I couldn't learn about it, or put its principles into use, fast enough in my life. I was so excited back then about the possibilities for myself and my family and, now that we have been living for several years based on those principles, its hard to find words substantial enough to tell you what a difference it has made. We have more energy and more fun. We get more done during the course of a day, and the quality of the work — from my work on the football field to Nureya's work in her own enterprises, tech development and catering — is greater. Our sleep at night is more restful. We *feel* better.

Functional medicine is a whole different and very new branch of medicine that deals with disease prevention. It tackles the causes that underlie serious, chronic disease rather than merely treating the symptoms but, even more important to the purpose that Julie and I have set for this book, it deals with *health*. *Wellness*. It teaches us how to prevent disease and injury by looking after our health *before* we get sick or have an accident.

I'm going to explain the six core principles of functional medicine in a way that I hope will make them easiest for you to share with your kids.

1. Health is not a "one size fits all" deal. What do I mean by that? Let's look at it in terms of what I

know best — football! Every play I run during a game is based on a practiced strategy. The playbook is filled with offensive and defensive tactics and schematics — and every player has to know them all. Are we trying to spread out the defense? Out of a Shotgun formation or from under center? Great; got it. How many potential blitzers are we dealing with? Three? Four? Five? *Why* are we running this particular play? To run the ball inside the tackles to get a numbers advantage? To get more receivers involved in a passing game? Are we running a modified pistol out of the Shotgun? And, critically, *what do we anticipate the defense will do in response? What scheme is the defense presenting? Which of our weaknesses will they try to attack?*

The play may be solid on paper, but making the play work depends on how well we players take all the variables into consideration.

In the same way, human biology might seem cut-and-dried, *on paper*— you can purchase a textbook and read all about it; we all have the same parts and they all have the same jobs to do in each body. But how the same body part works for you and for me and for the average twelve-year-old can be entirely different things.

Let's get past the obvious. I'm not talking just about the fact that my biceps are probably in every case going to be bigger and stronger than the average adolescent's. I'm not talking just about bones and muscles and hearts and livers. Functional medicine focuses, although not exclusively, on *biochemistry*— each person's totally unique mix of the natural human chemical components that sustain life: proteins and carbohydrates, peptides and acids and neurotransmitters and hormones and other such things. The way that this totally, individually unique chemical mix works for each person has everything to do with that person's genetic makeup, the speed of his or her personal metabolism, and the stresses that are specific to the environment in which that individual lives.

And when I say "environment" I don't mean only a person's physical surroundings — where they live and what that means in terms of the quality of food they can access or how near they live to the local power plant. In functional medicine the definition of "environment" includes their emotional environment. Is this kid having trouble with his grades? Does that kid have a tough home life? Is this other kid being bullied? These sorts of stresses on a child can have the same effect that grown-up stresses have on us: muscle pains, stomach upset and other digestive problems, immune system dysfunction, impaired lung function, high blood pressure, and abnormal heartbeat. Emotional turmoil can even cause skin problems — for example, stress can worsen acne!

Think of it this way: having a child who craves a healthy snack of apples and almonds may be what we think every parent dreams about, but for the parent of a child with a nut allergy it is the stuff of nightmares. While the idea of "nut allergy" (and the possible dire result of anaphylactic shock for someone with such an allergy who indulges) is widely accepted, and respected, the ability to tolerate or not tolerate nuts is but one of the myriad variations within each person's complex and nuanced and totally unique biochemical makeup.

2. "It is more important to know what patient has the disease than to know what disease the patient has." That's a quote from Sir William Osler, one of four founding professors of Johns Hopkins Hospital, and it is exactly the point from which functional medicine takes off. What it means is that taking care of the patient takes priority over taking care of the disease or injury. Let me illustrate with what you might think of as an obvious example. Say I've come up from the bottom of a pile during the fourth quarter with a swollen elbow. The first thing that's going to happen is the team trainer is going to put ice on that elbow. My teammate next to me came up from that same pile, but he took the stress on his knee. There's no reason to ice his elbow, right? The healing is all focused on his leg joint. When it comes to treating disease and healing injury, the road back to health is an easier trip when the doctor takes into consideration not just the obvious — knowing this guy's elbow from that guy's knee — but a patient's age, his general health, her activity level, as well as the patient's general mental and emotional circumstances. This is why a visit to a functional medicine practitioner includes an extensive interview with the patient *and* a thorough review of his medical history.

3. The body's biochemical balance is *dynamic*. That means it is always changing; therefore achieving the optimal balance for each individual body is

a day-by-day — and sometimes hour-by-hour or activity-by-activity — undertaking that is affected by both *internal and external factors.*

Pretend you're about to throw a football. How far and how accurately you can throw it depends on internal factors — how the muscles in your hand and arm contract to hold the ball and execute the toss — and external factors such as, for example, the weather. If it's raining, the ball may be slippery, or, if the day is sunny, the sun may get in your eyes, and so forth. Executing a good pass hinges on the interplay between your muscles contracting so you can grip the ball (internal factor) and the rain that's coming down (external factor), making both your hand and the ball slick. Your ultimate pass also depends on how well you can *adapt* when any of the factors change — the rain starts to come down harder, or your hand cramps, or some folks in the bleachers start chanting your name.

In just the same way, you need to be nimble in adjusting what your body, and your child's body, needs to stay in balance. For example, the body's need for vitamin C changes frequently, day to day, hour to hour. My needs on Tuesday during the season, when we rest our bodies, are very different than they are on Sunday afternoon when I'm going full out and taking hits. Vitamin C is a great antioxidant and, for that reason alone, it should be part of your healthy daily diet and/or supplement routine. When your kid is in a situation, however, where she's experiencing more oxidative stress than usual — she's nervous about trying out for the school chorus, or he's facing a big test, or she came home from school with the sniffles and you know she's getting sick — her body needs more vitamin C in order to cope.

4. Normal human life — a grown-up's life or a kid's — is filled with challenges that change from day to day. The nutrients (foods and supplements) as well as the amount of exercise we need to meet those tests with both peak physical ability and mental clarity fluctuate with every new challenge. The human body is like a well-trained, coordinated offense. As you couldn't really have a game without a center to snap the ball, a quarterback to receive it, tackles to block, running backs to carry, or wide receivers to catch passes, all of the organs and other structures of the human body have to work together in a coordinated way for the body to perform with real agility and vigor. If a body doesn't get enough nutrients in its belly, the brain doesn't think as well; air pollution impacts not just our lungs but such things as our hormonal function, and it also plays a role in low birth rates among infants; flossing your teeth can help to keep your heart healthy and your immune system functioning more competently. When I'm on the field with my team, my quarterback can do a bang-up job calling the play and targeting an open receiver, but if I don't do my job well, he could get sacked before the ball is out of his hands. Same thing with the human body — all the separate parts need to be in good working order for the whole to score a win.

5. Good health can't be described only by the absence of disease. What I mean is, you can't define "health" in negative terms because, by its very definition, "health" is a positive quality.

   What if, for example, I tried to describe my team's last game in the negative? "Well, we didn't lose." Worse, what if the team *played* the game with the intent of merely "not losing"? We could, theoretically, I suppose, skate by, getting a three- or six- or- seven-point lead and then phoning it in just enough to make sure the other team didn't score against us again, expending the minimum amount of energy and thought and care needed for us to eke out a victory. That would make for some sluggish, boring football, wouldn't it? And, if the team didn't care enough to do its best, why would the fans? On the other hand, when we strive to win — when we give the best of ourselves to what we're doing — the fans get what they want, and what they deserve.

   Winning isn't a matter of simply not losing — it is all about playing as hard and smart as you can. Being healthy isn't a matter of simply not being sick — it's about having a vital reserve, about having what you need to *be able* to play as smart and hard as you can.

6. This final principle of functional medicine may be the most difficult to explain. In a nutshell, the principle is that *promotion of organ reserve enhances health span*. But let's break it down so we can all understand it.

   When I say "organ reserve" what I'm talking about is the ability of our organs to sustain and support life. For me, the off season is a time to create the reserve I'm going to need to get my brain and my body through an entire season — playing as well in Week Sixteen as I do in Week One. The better I do at creating the reserve, the easier it is to maintain it during the season.

As children, our organs have the capacity to do much more work than our small bodies need them to do. That's a big part of why kids and younger people can take a health hit and come back from it so much more efficiently than older folks can. As we get older, and our bodies are exposed to the cumulative effects of aging — maybe a diet that isn't as rich in nutrients as it could have been, or years of lack of exercise, or a lifetime at a job that exposed us to environmental toxins — our organs are pushed, over and over again, to their limits. The reserves that we enjoyed as children begin to be depleted and our organs begin to do their jobs under stress.

Fortunately, there's a lot we can do to remedy, and even reverse, that stress. A regular routine of taking good quality supplements is a good example of what we can do to remedy the reserve problem — and I'm not talking about just getting the "daily value" that is typically printed on the labels of most vitamin brands. The "daily value" isn't what your body needs in order to be able to function at peak capacity; the daily value is *only the minimum required in order for you not to get sick as a result of a vitamin or mineral deficiency*. And, remember, the amount of a particular vitamin you need can change from day to day, situation to situation. Think football again for a moment. There are eleven players on each team on the field for any given play. But if there are only eleven players on the *whole team*, what happens when one of the eleven twists an ankle and there isn't a reserve player to send in to take his place? Would the game continue with just ten players? Could it continue? Like a football team needs more than eleven total players, your body needs more than the minimum dose of daily nutrients, so that your organs can build up the reserve they need to sustain and support you in the event of illness or injury.

6

OXIDATIVE STRESS AND CHRONIC INFLAMMATORY RESPONSE

 *" As complicated as medicine can be, no matter what goes wrong, the ultimate origins of the trouble are pretty elemental. "*

When we look at our health — and the health of our children — through the lens of functional medicine, it becomes crystal clear that we can't "compartmentalize" — our brains don't work separately from our hearts from our muscles from our liver from our stomach any more than a center can go alone onto a basketball court and play every position by himself. The center's role is vital, but, let's face it, he needs someone to tip the ball *to*. She needs her team to pass and assist and shoot.

With this new view on health, then, a new way to look at disease as well as injury emerges: at their roots they are the result of cells that are malfunctioning somewhere in the body. Bob Rountree, MD, a functional medicine practitioner and Institute for Functional Medicine faculty member, has gone so far as to say that when we understand that the body is truly restorative, that it wants to be healthy and whole, we have to also understand that there really is no such thing as disease, only a failure of the body to restore itself. The challenge, then, in preventing and healing disease — as well as in preventing and healing injury — is to get and to keep our cells at their optimum performance levels *before* we get sick or get hurt. In the most basic example, an athlete who is in top physical shape when she falls and breaks a leg is going to have a much easier time during recovery than someone who spends her days at a desk job, eats fast food for two out of three meals a day, and thinks of the walk from her car to her front porch as exercise.

I am not saying that we all need to train as hard as an NBA player in order to take a preventative approach to our health — nothing of the sort; most of us don't use our bodies every day as hard as elite athletes use theirs. We do, however, need to take a page from their playbooks and understand that by training ourselves and our kids to form healthy habits, we can do our own jobs — and live our whole lives — with more energy and relish. And then, when we do face illness or injury, our bodies will be in the position to restore themselves more quickly.

I'm also not saying — and I want to make this point very clear — that in using the principles of functional medicine to guide our health, we bypass the treatments that traditional, Western medicine offers. Functional medicine vigorously embraces those tools and their appropriate use in restoring and maintaining health. You break a leg, you take yourself to a hospital and have that leg x-rayed, set, and put in a cast. What I am saying is that bones that were healthy before the break happened — and that continue to be well-nourished through diet and benefit from other alternative therapies during recovery — are going to heal more thoroughly, and more quickly, and the injured person is going to have an altogether easier time bouncing back from that broken limb.

Most every doctor and health care professional — even the ones who aren't well versed in the principles of functional medicine — will agree with this concept. For example, nearly thirty years ago, a friend was hit by a car while out on her daily jog. It was a bad accident — broken bones, punctured organs; eleven weeks and nine different surgeries later she was finally able to go home from the hospital and start rehab in earnest. On the day she was released, her primary physician — a doctor who'd gone to medical school in the 1950s and was, as you might expect, fairly "old school" in his medical practice — told her family that it was a blessing that my friend was in good physical shape when she got hit because she had the strong constitution it took to survive the sort of injuries she had sustained.

Evidence-based medicine (EBI) is discussed as the practice of medicine that focuses, in part, on using the observations of well-designed clinical studies and other research to inform the decisions of the health care professional. But that's a narrow interpretation of a much broader definition. From the time of Hippocrates, before there were clinical studies, we clinicians have relied upon what we know from clinical practice — from what we have observed about how our patients respond and react. While studies and research abound, it's important to note that just because something has been published, it's not definitively a well designed study or piece of research! And, frankly, there isn't a doctor worth his salt who is going to tell you its just as easy to heal a patient who takes care of her daily health as it is to help one who does not. So be sure to understand that in addition to the clinical trials, the rest of the definition of evidence-based medicine includes this accumulated clinical wisdom we all employ when we walk into a room to care for our patients.

Health is not simply the absence of disease or function, it is a reserve of vital capacity — a reserve that comes in mighty handy when you're facing illness or recovery from an injury.

BEFORE WE GO on, I want to talk about two ways in which, during the course of day-to-day living, our bodies are routinely insulted — and the good habits that can help to mitigate these insults. These mechanisms are *oxidative stress* and *chronic inflammatory response*.

Oxidative Stress. I know that my own kids, when they were younger, probably talked — disparagingly — between themselves about how I *nagged* them to put their bikes away in the garage. Now that they're older, they understand why I nagged them. The bikes could be stolen if they were left outside at night. Their father or I could run over a bike left in the driveway, damaging both the bike and the family car. And bikes left out in the weather, exposed to too much wind and rain and sun, could rust.

Rust is the upshot of a chemical reaction called *oxidation*. What happens during the process of oxidation is that electrons are removed from atoms and molecules in the metal because of their interaction with too much oxygen. When these electrons are removed, it causes the corrosion we commonly refer to as rust.

We aren't made of metal, of course, so oxygen isn't generally a problem for humans — but our bodies can "rust" too. How in the world can that be?

To create the energy our bodies need to function — to work and play and live our daily lives — we eat food. After we digest food, it is turned into fuel through the process of *metabolism*, and it is combined with the air that we breathe through a specific part of the metabolic process called *catabolism*. But this process of creating the fundamental fuel we need has a downside. Catabolism also creates largely unwanted, and even potentially dangerous, byproducts known as *free radicals*.

Free radicals are, in the most kid-friendly terms, incomplete things, a puzzle missing a critical piece — technically they are electronically unstable atoms. They are "unstable" because they don't have all the electrons they need to be a complete, or "stable", unit — a three-legged stool with only two legs, so to speak. The thing is, they desperately want to be stable and complete. In order to try to make themselves complete they bounce around in the body as out of control as a six-year old hopped up on high fructose corn syrup[1] after a soda binge, randomly grabbing electrons from the body's stable atoms. But what happens when they swipe one of their missing electrons from a stable atom is that they make that formerly complete atom incomplete and unstable. Free radicals raid healthy cells and, in the process, create more and more free radicals as they go about their scavenging. In short, the process of stealing electrons breaks down the structures of the healthy cells that are robbed, leaving those cells damaged and unable to play their part in sustaining life.

Digesting food, however, isn't the only way that free radicals are created. They are also the result of *environmental stressors*. And what, exactly, are environmental stressors? Well, they're the toxins in the food we eat — such as the petrochemical fertilizers that have been commonly used in agribusiness since the 1950s to grow our fruits and vegetables. They're the pollutants in the water we drink — such as sulfur dioxide discharge from power plants, ammonia

1 http://www.salon.com/2015/01/04/coke_made_us_all_obese_mcdonalds_high_fructose_corn_syrup_
and_the_sick_super_sized_strategy_to_make_you_fat/.

discharge from food processing plants, and heavy metals discharged from car exhausts that get into our water supply by way of urban storm-water runoff. They're in the air we breathe — for example, *particulate matter*, which is made up of the hundreds of different chemicals emitted by smokestacks, construction sites, and motor vehicles.

In fact, environmental stressors are all around us, every day, in nearly every commonplace thing we touch: the BPAs in our plastic water bottles — and in the water we drink from them, the hormone disruptors in the liquid antiseptic soaps we use to wash hands, the aluminum in many deodorants, the amalgams in our dental fillings, the chemicals in household cleaning products, and in the fertilizers and weed killers used to keep our lawns — and our children's playing fields — green. While in the last ten or twenty years it has become much more widely known within the general population that the chemicals in everyday products are harmful to us in a myriad of terrible ways — a quick, random Google search netted this article about birth defects that have been linked to glyphosate, the "chemical at the heart of the planet's most widely used herbicide, Roundup weedkiller"[1] — regulation of such dangerous substances remains elusive; it is nearly impossible to avoid coming into contact with some sort of environmental stress factor in the course of modern life.

This constant bombardment of toxins is one of the reasons that it's important for everyone — for our kids and for us grown-ups as well — to make sure we get not only adequate but liberal doses of Vitamins C and E. These vitamins in particular can counter some of the effects of oxidative stress because they are "donors" — literally offering some of their electrons to the free radicals and

---

1 http://www.huffingtonpost.com/2011/06/24/roundup-scientists-birth-defects_n_883578.html.

stabilizing them, thus repairing some of the damage that toxins have caused and often preventing cellular "suicide", an act our cells are programmed to perform if they are too damaged to recover.

Here's the thing: I don't think any of us can get an optimum amount of necessary nutrients just from eating food in this day and age. That's due in large part to the modern farming methods that Big Agriculture uses to grow our food, and the resulting dilution of the vitamins and minerals contained in that food. For example, the U.S. Department of Agriculture found that the calcium content of broccoli, which averaged 12.9 milligrams per one gram (dry weight) in 1950, had decreased, in 2003, to only 4.4 milligrams per one gram of dry weight. According to Dr. Donald Davis of the Biochemical Institute in the Department of Chemistry and Biochemistry at the University of Texas, "During [the past] fifty years, there have been intensive efforts to breed new varieties that have greater yield, or resistance to pests, or adaptability to different climates. But the dominant effort is for higher yields. Emerging evidence suggests that when you select for yield, crops grow bigger and faster, but they don't necessarily have the ability to make or uptake nutrients at the same, faster rate." The study, for which he is the lead author, found declines in nutrients including proteins, calcium, phosphorus, iron, riboflavin and ascorbic acid of between 6 to 38%.[2]

This is disquieting news, to say the least. When I went to medical school, the mantra was that a good healthy *balanced* diet was sufficient to maintain nutrient status. But between increased environmental stressors on our bodies, and diluted nutrient sources in our food, I'm not confident that just a healthy diet is sufficient for many of us anymore.

---

2 http://www.utexas.edu/news/2004/12/01/nr_chemistry/.

The solutions these days include consciously eating better by choosing organic produce, or even growing your own produce in a family, backyard garden. But what we buy and grow and consume needs to be bought and grown and eaten with forethought. The vitamin A needs to balance with the vitamin D, the calcium with the magnesium, the vitamin E with the vitamin K.

Taking good quality, targeted supplements on a routine basis can also be quite helpful.

Chronic Inflammatory Response. When we bang our shin against a table, slice a finger instead of the apple we were paring, or are exposed to a flu virus, our bodies respond with one of their most basic protective functions: the inflammatory response. This response sends cells and biochemicals to the site of the bruise, the cut, the cluster of foreign virus particles to do battle and begin the healing process. We can see, and often feel, the body's attempt to heal itself—redness, a localized warmth, swelling, even tiredness, bleeding and pain can be clues that our body's defenses have kicked in and are addressing the injury we have sustained or the disease that has invaded our system. This rush to defense is called an *acute inflammatory response*; it is immediate, beneficial, and short-lived.

A *chronic* inflammatory response, however, is what happens when the body's urge to repair itself goes into overdrive *because the insult it has sustained is, or is perceived to be, continuous.* Here is a most amazing biological fact: the body won't stop trying to repair itself just because it hasn't yet been successful at the task. Its defense operations are diligent, and tenacious, but can be confused if they aren't immediately successful: when the inflammatory response is prolonged, the cells and biochemicals the body dispatches to tend to the insult can start to attack healthy cells and tissues, simultaneously healing and causing more damage.

Let's say, for example, that your kid is a baseball player and he scored the winning run for his Little League team by taking a flying leap and sliding into home base — on a rainy day. His nice, white, not-inexpensive baseball pants are caked with mud, and the mud has pretty much dried, the stain set, by the time you get home. You pull out a clean cloth and some solvent and begin to work on the stain and, at first, the stain begins to fade so you think your efforts to save the pants are paying off. The stain is stubborn, however, so you pour a little more solvent on it, rub a little harder. Eventually you may succeed at removing the stain, but at the cost of having treated the fabric so harshly that you've damaged the fibers, weakening their strength, changing their texture or color, or even making a hole in the garment.

In the body, the long-term effects of chronic inflammation are similar: the cells and tissues are weakened, their structures altered, and holes, or wounds, begin to appear in the tissue. And, when cells and tissues are compromised in this manner, we are more vulnerable to disease. This also creates a vulnerability to unforeseen injury!

As an example, let's talk about a little bacteria known as Helicobacter pylori, or H. pylori. It is estimated that nearly half of the world's population is currently infected with H. pylori, which grows only in the stomach, weakening its protective coating so that digestive juices begin to irritate the delicate stomach lining.[1] It is responsible for most ulcers and many cases of stomach inflammation, or what is also called chronic gastritis.[2] A 1994 study by the International Agency for Research on Cancer concluded that human

---

1 http://www.ncbi.nlm.nih.gov/pubmedhealth/PMH0001276/.
2 Ibid.

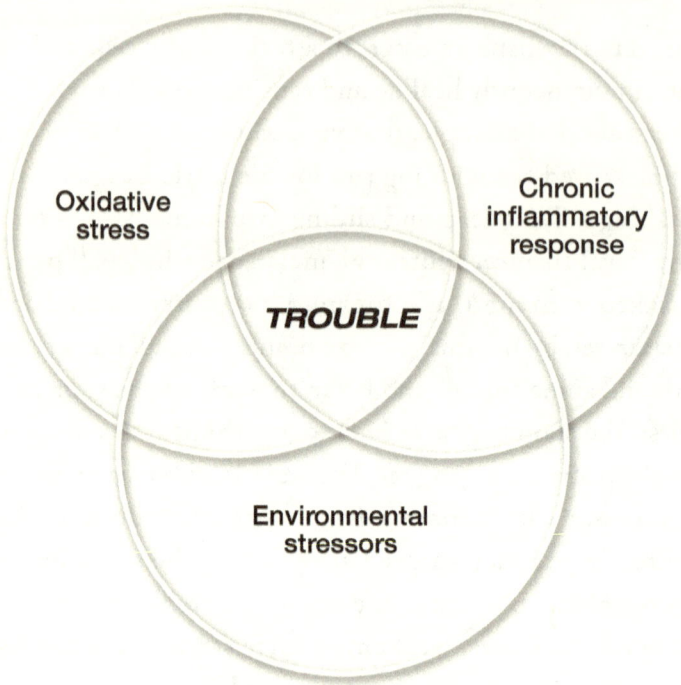

Oxidative stress

Chronic inflammatory response

TROUBLE

Environmental stressors

H. pylori infection is associated with the risk of developing adenocarcinoma (i.e., cancer) of the stomach, one of the most common malignancies in the world, as well as two other types of cancers.[1]

Think of it: one of every two people in the world is infected with potentially cancer-causing stomach bacteria. Chronic inflammation is everywhere and is such a silent epidemic. An alarming statistic is that over 50% of American adults and children are currently on some form of medication for chronic illness.[2] This includes almost two-thirds of women over twenty years of age, over half of adult men, three in four adults over sixty-five, and *one in four children and teens*.[3]

---

1 http://www.cdc.gov/ncidod/eid/vol4no3/cassell.htm.

2 http://www.foxnews.com/story/0,2933,355540,00.html.

3 Ibid.

CHRONIC INFLAMMATORY RESPONSE and oxidative stress are both contributors to and evidence of disease processes in our bodies — this, science knows for sure. And we also know that developing good habits, taking care of ourselves, can reverse the negative health impacts of these conditions — and that if we develop these habits early enough in life, we can keep from developing these conditions in the first place. When it comes to young athletes, we really have to step up how we manage these conditions. That's because athletes — even our youngest ones — are pushing themselves as hard as they can to learn new physical skills and win games. Pushing as hard as they can to learn and excel is good for kids, of course, but it's also a form of stress — physical, mental, emotional stress. Think of it as a Venn diagram: where oxidation, chronic inflammation, and environmental stressors meet is where trouble can start to happen. The great news is that both of these conditions can largely be controlled with a good diet.

7

PREVENTION IS ALL ABOUT HEALTHY HABITS

" Developing healthy habits can be the hardest thing you'll ever try to do—at least until you start to feel better…"

I think it's fair to say that parents have never had it easy — I know my mom didn't, and since I've become a parent myself I have a whole new appreciation for the love, the thought, the energy, the time, the patience, and the money it takes to grow a child.

But even back in the late '90s and early 2000s, when I was playing youth sports, we either didn't have the kind of medical information we have today or that information wasn't as readily available. Moms and dads didn't feel badly about — probably didn't even think twice about — sending the kids off to school with a sandwich of processed meat on white bread, a thermos of chocolate milk, and a Hostess cupcake for dessert. My mother and other parents like her were not educated on the direct impact nutrition plays on athletic — and scholastic — performance. These days, as a society, we're more aware of the dangers in things like trans fats, bleached and gluten-packed flours, and all things sugar, than ever before. We know that those things are bad for our kids — for all of us — even if it's still hard to avoid eating them.

Bad foods are hard to avoid, first of all, because our food supply system in this country is so compromised. We have these grocery stores that stretch out for what seem like acres, packed with processed foods on every aisle, and maybe only a sixth or seventh of the available food space given over to fresh vegetables and fruits and whole proteins. Even in the produce and meat sections, though, you have to be careful about what you buy because the vegetables are probably grown with chemical pesticides and the meat is raised with the use of hormones and antibiotics — and if we eat those foods the pesticides and antibiotics just become part of what is on our dinner plates. *Bad food is mostly what is available to us.* In some, mostly urban, areas of the country, bad food is *all* that's available — places like these, where all consumers can get their hands on are frozen dinners and bags of potato chips and coolers filled with soda, are called *food deserts*.

The second reason it's so hard to keep our kids from eating bad foods is because that's just about the only kind served at most school cafeterias. Though cafeteria food has improved by leaps and bounds from where it was even ten or fifteen years ago when I was in school, check out the lunch menu posted online for your kid's school; while you're likely going to see more servings of fruits and vegetables than you did back when you were in school yourself, my bet is that the bulk of the food served is greasy 'Cheesy Breadsticks', French bread pizza, or some sort of pasta — all made with processed, bleached, enriched, and gluten-packed flours that have been stripped, by way of chemical processes, of whatever nutritional value they might have originally possessed. The passing nod to protein on these menus is often nothing more than deep-fried chicken nuggets or a slice of processed ham thrown in with the grilled cheese sandwich.

But here's the real problem: though most of us know the basic principles for eating better, it doesn't really occur to us that most of the food offered to us in our schools and supermarkets is garbage. It doesn't occur to us because of the simple fact that it's *in* our supermarket and in our schools. It's *labeled* as 'food'. Everyone else eats that 'food'. The media — especially commercials — tell us the 'food' tastes good, and that it's good for us. We often have to go out of our way, and pay more, for real food, and then we have to argue with our kids — our picky or independent eaters — to get them to eat it...

In the moment it can just seem so much easier not to bother. To give in.

But then we get right back to where I started — being a parent just isn't an easy job any way you cut it. And living in a culture where our food is produced by big agribusiness that has no concern for our health, and where our health is overseen by physicians who aren't trained adequately to understand that our diet is the primary — *fundamental* — way in which we can preserve and protect our health, well, that doesn't make a parent's job any easier.

In this section of the book, Julie and I are going to lay out three principle ways in which you can help your children look after their fundamental health, so that when they do get sick or sustain an injury, they'll have the reserve they need to recover fully and as quickly as possible. We'll also give you some good ideas to get your kids invested in their own health so they'll cooperate not just willingly, but happily, in their own well being. Because, as parents, we all know that a little cooperation can make any job that much easier.

*"*Turns out, Grandma did know best.*"*

The three principle areas to focus on to help your kids grow up strong and healthy — and your youth athletes stay strong and healthy — are pretty darned basic:

- Diet. Make sure they get lots of good, whole *real* foods, and that they drink plenty of water.
- Exercise. Make sure they get some physical activity every day, preferably in an outdoor setting.
- Sleep. An adult may be able to get away with six to seven hours a night, however bad an idea it is to shortchange oneself on sleep; kids need so much more sleep time.

Sounds simple, right? Let's break it all down and get to the nuances.

8

NUTRITION, SUPPLEMENTS, AND HYDRATION

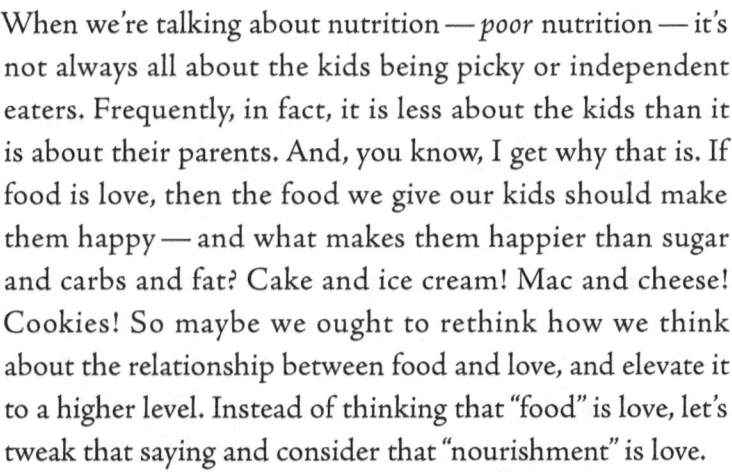

"❝If you're going to let it cross your lips, make sure you really want it in your body. Whatever it is, your gut will try to turn it into you.❞

When we're talking about nutrition — *poor* nutrition — it's not always all about the kids being picky or independent eaters. Frequently, in fact, it is less about the kids than it is about their parents. And, you know, I get why that is. If food is love, then the food we give our kids should make them happy — and what makes them happier than sugar and carbs and fat? Cake and ice cream! Mac and cheese! Cookies! So maybe we ought to rethink how we think about the relationship between food and love, and elevate it to a higher level. Instead of thinking that "food" is love, let's tweak that saying and consider that "nourishment" is love.

The ultimate food of love is breast milk. It is a miracle elixir. If you taste it, it tastes different every day, and it also tastes different throughout each feeding process. The foremilk — the milk the baby gets at the beginning of her meal — has a high water content, and is high in lactose, as well as water-soluble proteins and vitamins. Babies are generally thirsty at the beginning of a feeding, and the high water content serves to appease the baby's thirst and keep her well-hydrated. The hindmilk, on the other hand, is rich in fat, which the baby needs to gain weight, and for brain development. Breast milk is the ultimate love, the ultimate food, the ultimate *nourishment.*

Why is it that after a child is no longer dining on breast milk, we lower the standards of the food we offer to him? Maybe it's because we don't often know — or if we know, we don't *remember*— that the things our culture calls "food" are often not really food at all.

And we parents aren't the only ones who don't know. I believe wholeheartedly that annual well visits with a pediatrician are the best way to check in on our children's health. But I have a problem with how most of them are conducted. First of all, most of them last an average of eighteen minutes. Think about that — you have the opportunity just a few times a year, or, depending on your child's age, only once a year, to focus on your child's health with her doctor, and all you get is eighteen minutes? That's barely enough time to get through the basics: checking height and weight and blood pressure, and listening to the child's heart and lungs. There needs to be good communication during a physical exam between patient and doctor, and you can't address all the issues that need to be attended to in an eighteen-minute physical — especially when someone else comes in to take the patient's history, and someone else again comes in to take the vitals, and the doctor appears for a whole seven minutes of the allotted eighteen.

Your child's well visit should include time for her doctor to do things like watching her play with blocks or ask her a few simple life questions to observe if her developmental skills are on track. It should include time for you to ask, and

Julie Makes the Case for Casein-free Kids

Well, both Eugene and I make the case for removing (or, at least, really, *really* limiting!) milk and milk products from your kid's diet within this chapter. However, I wanted to take a brief time out to tell you a little more about *casein*. The word "casein" is derived from Latin for the word "cheese," and encompasses, in the parlance of modern chemistry, the whole family of related *phosphoproteins*, which are the type of proteins commonly found in mammal's milk. They make up about 85% of the proteins found in cow's milk, the variety of mammal's milk we humans have grown most used to drinking and consuming in ice cream, yogurt, and other milk products. As a comparison, that's 300% more casein than is found in human milk!

One of the chemical uses of casein—besides as part of dairy products intended for human consumption—is to make some of the strongest *glue* products in the world. That may sound slightly creepy—that what has become one of our major dietary components is also used to make glue—but it is also very relevant when we talk about why we shouldn't be eating it. Because of the high amount of casein in milk and other dairy products, it is super good at manufacturing mucus, which is, as we all know, really good for clogging and irritating our respiratory systems. Clogged and irritated respiratory systems, in turn, cause or exacerbate ailments and allergies, like hay fever, asthma, and bronchitis—and, if you or your kid currently suffers from the common allergy of lactose intolerance, you're already an expert in the sort of acute havoc casein can cause in the human body. And please don't even think about drinking it when you've got a cold or an ear infection unless you want to sniffle and sneeze and cough for an even longer period of time.

Another reason to avoid casein is that it can, in certain individuals, increase the production of cerebral folate autoantibodies. This can significantly impact the function of brain neurotransmitters and cells in a negative way. Removing casein in some individuals can decrease rage, improve mood, sharpen focus, and heighten cognitive function!

have satisfactorily answered, any questions you might bring to the table. Why is my three-year-old still wetting the bed? Why is my eight-year-old having trouble concentrating on schoolwork? How can I get my twelve-year-old interested again in basic human hygiene?

It should include plenty of time for the doctor to talk with and interact with both kids and their parents because this is the best opportunity your doctor has to assess the child's health in a holistic way, and discover the sorts of developmental issues or injuries that might otherwise be overlooked. This includes injuries they may have sustained — and that may not yet have been detected — while they were playing sports. These sorts of common, hidden injuries include stress fractures to young, soft bones, "Little League Elbow" that refers to damage to the cartilage in the elbow and is caused by repetitive throwing motion, and alignment problems in the knee that can cause grinding of the bones and, in time, damage to the joints, cartilage — and, eventually, adult arthritis. And, of course, hidden injuries include damage to the brain that can happen whenever a child is hit, even just once, in the head with a flying baseball, crashes just once against the wall of a pool, or goes down in the middle of a tackle on the football field.

Unfortunately, detecting these sorts of injuries often requires specialized training, and most well-child visits don't allow sufficient time to truly evaluate such injuries — or to recommend either the therapeutic techniques to heal them, or the training techniques that could have prevented them in the first place. Talk to your child's doctor about the sport your kid plays, his sports-related activities, history, and goals. Find out about your doctor's background and training in sports medicine, and his or her overall philosophy about preventative care for youth athletes.

Doctors who take the pressures of youth sports seriously will also understand how important it can be to do blood work on a regular — at least annual — basis. Why is blood analysis so important for kids, especially young athletes? Well, for one thing, a blood test can tell you if your child is anemic — and a full 9% of kids, almost on in ten, in the US are.[1] And as unbelievable as it is, many of them are female athletes. Anemia is the body's lack of healthy red blood cells that carry oxygen to the body's tissues. Because iron is necessary for the body to create red blood cells, and children can absorb only a small amount of the iron they eat, the lack of iron is the most common cause of the problem. Happily, it can be easily remedied by diet and dietary supplements — indeed, most kids with iron deficiencies can have blood counts again within the normal range within two months of starting treatment; the issue is that the problem has to be found before it can be treated, and discovery requires suspicion that there's a problem, and a blood test.

It is also important to look at liver function. Because of the turnover of muscle that athletes experience, the liver is working overtime and it is important to optimally support the liver while it's working so hard. Milk thistle, or silybum marianum, an herb, is an effective supplement if the child's blood test shows that his liver could use the help.

Tests to help you and your doctor to understand how the mitochondria, the energy generators inside of each individual cell, are functioning are relatively challenging to perform and evaluate. Mitochondria are what fuel our cells and allow them to perform all the functions that sustaining life requires. I like to think of mitochondria as the oil refinery of the cell. They take whatever form of crude

1   http://www.cdc.gov/nchs/fastats/anemia.htm.

fuel is presented to them, be it protein, carbohydrate animal fat, or the healthy fats from nuts and seeds, and turn that crude into refined fuel in a form the body can use — ATP, or adenosine tri-phosphate. Evaluating mitochondrial function with blood work is not easy, but we can look at the ratio between liver function tests pretty easily. Specifically, in this test, the ratio of AST: ALT should be under 2:1 if mitochondria are functioning optimally. Although it's a much longer and much more detailed conversation if there are significant concerns about mitochondrial function, in general, healthy fat, Co-Q10, and carnitine will support mitochondria and fuel production if they are not functioning optimally.

Blood tests will also reveal your child's cholesterol level. As adults, we're used to worrying about our cholesterol being too high but, for kids, often the focus should be on it being too *low*. What's that, you say? Too *low*? Yes. Kids need cholesterol in order to build their brains and your doctor should pay attention to your child's level of it.

An annual physical exam should also, importantly, include a detailed evaluation of the child's nutrition, but these sorts of concentrated dietary evaluations are almost non-existent. That's because most physicians are poorly educated about nutrition — and very rare is the doctor who has an understanding of both pediatric nutrition and what it takes to fuel a child who is also an athlete. Most practitioners have yet to elevate the role of nutrition in the maintenance of health to its rightful place. This has a lot to do with the fact that the subject of nutrition usually isn't given adequate weight in medical school. And even if it were, most physicians don't have adequate time during the visit to adequately address this topic. Happily, doctors themselves, as well as medical students, are starting to notice this — "You can't just keep writing out script after script after script of new medications when diet is just as important as drugs or any other treatment a patient may be using," says Katherine Chauncey, a professor of clinical family medicine at Texas Tech and registered dietician.[1] Thankfully, the way in which we educate doctors about nutrition is starting to change, if ever so slowly.

Ideally, your pediatrician understands that a good diet is the primary ingredient in helping children grow strong, both physically and mentally, and will recognize the importance of taking the time to help his patients grow up embracing this understanding themselves. Critically, he will know that, at the first sign that something is amiss in your child's health, he should be talking extensively about food that nourishes and where deficiencies are in the child's diet. But this is not yet Standard Operating Procedure in most of our traditional medical settings. Until then, it falls to us parents ourselves to ask the questions and do the research that will benefit our kids, and help to educate medical professionals.

It goes without saying that of all the people who don't know how our children should eat, the children themselves are at the top of the list. A lot of that is because what they know is all over the place. Fast food joints line the main thoroughfares of our towns and suburbs. Their advertisers, ubiquitous on the very programming kids love most, employ cozy mascots to tempt our children with fat- and salt- and sugar-laden junk. School cafeterias offer teeth-rotting sodas in vending machines, and greasy, carb-heavy fare in the lunch line. The peer pressure our kids face when it comes to food can easily be likened to the adult pressure to have an alcoholic beverage when out to dinner with friends

---

1   http://www.nytimes.com/2010/09/16/health/16chen.html?_r=0.

or at the office holiday party. Moreover, junk food is cheap; for independent, fuel-hungry teenage eaters on a budget, eking every penny from the paychecks at their first jobs, being able to buy a "full meal" for five bucks is a big, "drive-thru" draw. How can parents fight back and teach their kids that fast food isn't really food at all? And even more importantly, how do we teach ourselves that fast "food" is far from cost effective, either nutritionally or financially?

The most significant way in which we parents can impact our children's food choices is the same way we can best influence everything they do: through example. We all worry that kids are going to pick up the bad habits we demonstrate for them — for example, kids who grow up in homes where the grown-ups smoke are more likely to smoke themselves[1] — but with all the worry we sometimes forget that they also pick up our good habits. If we serve healthy food in our homes, and make healthy choices for ourselves when we take our kids out to a restaurant, that's what they are going to learn to do for *themselves*, too. I have been preaching to what is now my own personal choir — my own two kids as well as my patients — since they were quite little or first walked into my office, so I was pleased but not surprised when my son came home from middle school and told me this story. He'd pulled out his container of yummy left-over, veggie-rich stir-fry at lunchtime and his friend, whose mom had just dropped off some Mexican-style fast "food" for her own kiddo, pulled out his beefy burrito with "cheese" sauce. His friend looked at my son's lunch, wrinkled his nose and said, "Why are you eating that?" To which Matt replied, watching the grease congeal around his friend's "cheese" sauce, "A much better question

1   http://www.nbcnews.com/health/kids-health/when-parents-smoke-more-so-do-their-kids-n101601

is why are you eating *that?*" My point is that modeling the behavior you want your children to emulate *works*.

Teaching young people about food is, actually, one of my favorite things to do. I think the first time I did it — outside of talking to my young patients in my office when their parents bring them into for well visits — was for a unit my son's Boy Scout troop was doing on nutrition. I took the boys to the grocery store and conducted the whole lesson there, giving them some ground rules and then letting them spread out into the store to shop for the food they would take camping. Those early ground rules remain the foundation for how I talk to kids about food. Here's what I say to them:

1. First thing to ask yourself when you're choosing food is, "Do I have to open a package in order to eat it?" A package is, in many cases, a dead giveaway that whatever is inside contains a lot of chemical preservatives. Chemical preservatives are used by "food" manufacturers to retain the color or flavor of their products, as well as to inhibit mold and delay the growth of microorganisms that cause decay. Packaged food commonly contains preservatives called benzoates, nitrites, or sulphites. These preservatives have been linked to everything from allergic reactions to cancer to birth defects. You definitely do not want your kid snacking on them.

2. The second thing you want to ask yourself about your food is, "Is it colorful?" Eating a rainbow is an approach that focuses on what we should eat rather than what we should not eat, and it has real kid appeal. Eating your colors — the colors that Mother

Nature gave the food, not the colors added by a factory — is especially important when we're talking about making sure we have enough anti-oxidants — foods that help us combat those pesky free radicals. There are three types of antioxidants we can get from the foods we eat — carotenoids, isothiocyanates, and flavonoids, though there's no need to be a chemistry professor to know which ones we're getting from which foods. All you have to do is eat by color!

Carotenoids are of two types — oxygen-containing molecules like lutein, also known as xanthophylls, and, even better known, the oxygenated molecules called carotenes, as in beta-carotene. You get beta-carotene from yellow and orange foods like pineapples and yellow squash. You get lutein from green, leafy vegetables such as spinach and kale. And from foods like tomatoes, watermelon, and mangos you get dense supplies of lycopene, a chemical that helps your body to put the antioxidants in carotenoids to their best use.

Isothiocyanate, thought to be responsible for helping to cart cancerous cells out of the body, is the chemical that is responsible for the green color and particular aroma of cruciferous veggies like dark green lettuces, broccoli, and Brussels sprouts, as well as a few white vegetables like cabbage and cauliflower.

Flavinoids are found in brightly colored food — red cabbage, raspberries, and purple grapes — as well as in tree fruits such as bananas and grapefruit, teas, dark chocolates, and fresh herbs such as dill and thyme. These chemicals have anti-oxidant as well as anti-cancer and anti-viral properties. If you're looking for a delicious way to tempt your kids to eat more foods that contain flavinoids, try this little trick. As flash-frozen fruits and vegetables often have more nutritional value than those picked ahead of their time and left to ripen on the long truck trip from farm to your grocer's produce aisle, pick up a big bag of organic, flash-frozen blueberries or strawberries and keep them in your freezer. Serve your kiddos a bowl of vanilla-flavored coconut milk yogurt topped with a handful of the frozen berries for a quick breakfast. They'll think they're having a treat, but you'll know how good it is for them.

3. The third question to ask yourself when you're choosing food is, "What are the first three ingredients listed on the package?" Ingredients are listed on a package by volume — that is, the first ingredient is the main ingredient, or the one that makes up most of the volume of the food; a smaller amount of the second ingredient is used, and an even smaller amount of the third is used, and so on down the list. Now, these days, manufacturers tend to add a lot of sugar to a lot of different foods, even ones that are already sweet all on their own, because consumers tend to buy sweet foods. If one of the first three ingredients is "sugar" or any of the other words that "food" manufacturers use to disguise the amount of sugar in their products, that product contains too much sugar.

What are some of the words to watch out for? *Sugar*— which can also be described as beet sugar, cane sugar, raw sugar, turbinado sugar, palm sugar, coconut sugar, brown sugar, cane crystals, cane juice crystals, or corn sweetener. *Syrup*— corn syrup, high-fructose corn syrup, glucose-fructose syrup, rice syrup, maple syrup, malt syrup, sorghum syrup, or corn syrup solids. Healthier sounding words like *honey, molasses, agave nectar,* or *fruit juice concentrate.* Any word ending with the letters "*ose*" such as glucose, fructose, dextrose, or xylose. And don't be fooled if the label says the food contains something like "organic palm sugar" — even if it's organic, it is still sugar, plain and simple.

4. The fourth question to ask yourself is, "Are more than the last three ingredients on the product label chemicals?" Because the manufacturer needs only a small amount of a chemical preservative to keep the food from rotting in its package, these and any other chemical ingredients are usually listed nearer to the bottom of the ingredient list. Ideally there will be no chemicals in the foods we choose, but a starting point is to minimize them by decreasing the numbers that we are willing to tolerate bringing into our homes and ultimately our bodies. You probably won't be able to easily pronounce the names of these chemicals, and that brings me to a great, general, *golden* rule: *if you can't pronounce it, don't eat it.*

I am a huge eater. I love food, and pretty much always have. I tried to learn how to cook when I was just five years old — I was hungry and Mom wasn't home, so I put some hot dogs on the stove. And then I forgot about them. I smoked everyone out of the house, and the fire department came... It was some time before I was allowed back in the kitchen. Fortunately, my grandmother cooked everyday and was patient — and brave — enough to teach me how to do it, too.

These days when I'm in the kitchen, though I still rely on some of the basic techniques my grandmother taught me — and without casting any aspersions on my grandmother's ability with food because she was a *really good cook*— I cook very differently than she did. But then, I expect that many of you deal with food differently than your grandmothers did. As an obvious example, most of us don't keep a block of lard or a can of Crisco as an everyday staple in the pantry. Most of us contemporary cooks roast and bake more often than we fry. We use more fresh or frozen vegetables rather than stocking our shelves with canned peas and corn. We're fluent with ingredients our grandparents probably had never heard of, like quinoa.

For me, however, the way we deal with food goes beyond techniques and whole, generally cleaner ingredients that would have surprised those in our grandparents' generation. My whole *philosophy* about food and cooking is different. I don't eat only because I'm hungry. I eat to fuel my body, so my body can perform at its peak level. As I said, I love food, and I'd even say my wife and I are "foodies". Heck, Nureya even has her own catering business.[1] But if the food I'm eating isn't good for me, I'm not enjoying it.

So, how does that philosophy translate into how I eat on a day-to-day basis?

Well, I suppose a fundamental part of it is that I eat like a baby. What I mean by that is a baby knows when it's feeding time. He listens to his body, knows what it is telling him he needs, and he asks for it. You grow up, however, and you start to ignore what your body is telling you. You start ignoring the messages it's sending you because it's inconvenient to stop what you're doing and take the time to get what you really want and need. Let's say you're on a road trip, and you start to crave a nice, juicy piece of chicken. That's your body crying out for protein, but the fueling station where you're gassing up your car has only a rack of bags filled with salty snacks, or a box of candy bars, so that's what you grab. The snack doesn't satisfy you — at least not for long — because your body is still lacking the nutrient that it wanted in the first place. All you've accomplished is to overload it with fat, salt, or sugar, and three to five hundred calories it didn't need. And when you don't give your body what it needs, that is when your body starts to break down — starts to lose its ability to perform, to run fast and react quickly and think clearly. This breakdown happens not after years of eating a poor diet, but mere *hours*. Think of it in these terms: if your car was out of gas when you pulled into that filling station, you'd fill it up with gas. Not water, not Pepsi, not V-8 juice. You'd give it what it needed to keep you on the road. And if you didn't, you probably wouldn't be surprised to find yourself stranded on the side of the road a few miles later. It is mind-blowing that people even consider taking better care of their car then they do of

1 http://goganics.net

their body, but that is what they do. The good news is that once you start to eat properly, to take preventative care of yourself, your body begins to immediately repair itself. So, even if you've reached the point of breakdown, you can take steps to start healing — and those steps will start to take effect right away.

A second fundamental part of how I eat is that I have completely given up milk and milk products — and the only milk my kids have ever had is breast milk. Look, in spite of all the press spin and dairy lobby advertising, milk is just a lousy source of calcium. Green, leafy vegetables and legumes are much better sources of this vital nutrient — the calcium in them is more absorbable by the body, for one thing; they are really what build strong bones and teeth. But it isn't just that dairy products aren't especially good for you that's worrisome, it is that they are actually *bad* for you that should be the greater concern. Milk consumption has been linked to breast cancer, prostate cancer, liver cancer, heart disease,[2] and even an increased likelihood of bone fracture![3] If you want to know more about the downside of milk, I highly recommend the book, *Don't Drink Your Milk*, by Frank A. Oski, MD, the former Chairman of the Department of Pediatrics at Johns Hopkins University School of Medicine, and Physician-in-Chief at the Johns Hopkins Children's Center.[4]

IT ISN'T ALWAYS easy to eat clean and healthy food. So I ask questions in restaurants and scout ahead of time for what's going to be available during away trips. What's in the sauce on the chicken? If the waiter doesn't know or can't

---

2 http://www.pcrm.org/health/cancer-resources/ask/ask-the-expert-dairy-products.

3 http://www.ncbi.nlm.nih.gov/pubmed/9224182.

4 http://www.amazon.com/Dont-Drink-Your-Milk-Frank/dp/1479601659/ref=sr_1_1?ie=UTF8&qid=1419
189303&sr=8-1&keywords=don%27t+drink+your+milk.

Julie Makes the Case for Gluten-free Kids

Gluten is a protein found in wheat and other grains such as rye, barley, and oats. It gives elasticity to dough, allowing it to rise and keep its shape, and providing a soft and chewy texture.

The Mayo Clinic estimates that Celiac disease, which is an immune reaction to eating gluten, is becoming "a major public health issue."[1] The diagnosis of celiac disease is four times more common today than it was only sixty years ago. It affects the health of about one in one hundred people.[2] We don't yet have a statistic on the number of people who have what is called "non-celiac gluten sensitivity"—a condition that doesn't cause an immune response but does cause gastrointestinal distress, skin problems such as rashes, joint pain, numbness of the hands and legs, generalized inflammatory response of cells, brain fog, and behavioral problems. But the suspicion is that one in every ten people have some level of gluten intolerance.

Science doesn't yet know why so many people are developing gluten sensitivities—why this particular allergic reaction is on the increase—but we do know how to combat it: eat a gluten-free diet. I came to the diet by way of autism. I had been using the diet for my own autistic child and recommending it to the parents of my patients with autism, long before science started proving it worked and accepting it as a viable treatment. All I had to go on was that it was working for my kid and my patients.[3] While bread may have been the staff of life several hundred years ago, the now genetically-modified wheat and grossly-increased gluten contained in it and other similar grain products is starting to wreak havoc on the gastrointestinal functions of modern-day men, women—and kids.

While those without gluten-specific symptoms may opt-in on certain gluten-containing products—Eugene enjoys oats, although he prefers

1 http://www.mayo.edu/research/discoverys-edge/celiac-disease-rise.
2 http://celiac.nih.gov/FAQ.aspx.
3 http://www.sciencedaily.com/releases/2012/02/120229105128.htm.

to consume them gluten free, for example—I believe that the less gluten we consume, the healthier we will be, and will remain, simply because less gluten translates to less inflammatory response in the cells of the body. Sometimes doing this is simple: using rice flour, for instance, instead of wheat flour when we crust our chicken. Sometimes it's harder—I'm talking about baked goods, here—but with folks who have a medical reaction to gluten on the rise, so are gluten-free food options. You can now buy commercially pre-packed mixes for wholesome, organic, gluten-free cakes and muffins and brownies that are so scrumptious and light, even a truly persnickety pastry chef would be hard-pressed to tell the difference.

As I said, I came to embrace both the gluten-free and casein-free approaches to eating through the treatment of autism patients; look in the Resources section of this book for more information about learning how to feed your children and family differently.

find out, I don't eat it. Am I going to be able to get healthy food when I'm on the road with my team? Am I going to be able to get the sort of fuel I need to play my best game when I get out on the field? If I won't be able to get the fuel I need, I throw some ice packs in a crushable cooler and take my own.

The intensity with which I'm recommending that you focus on your kid's diet may seem over-the-top to some, but what you eat — as well as what you *don't* eat — is the primary factor in realizing potential. Your kid may train like a maniac to make the team, and she may get a little stronger, or a little faster, but her body won't realize the *full* benefits of all of that work unless she gives it the right fuel.

On game days — depending on the NFL schedule, though the standard is a one o'clock game — I wake up and eat food that is going to give me the most energy. I keep it simple: gluten-free oatmeal, fruit, and a lean protein. Then I take my supplements with a protein shake, usually with added greens — spinach and kale are my favorites.

For lunch, I have already scouted out healthy options, like the boneless, skinless chicken breasts that the NFL offers as an option, and bring my own vegetables and gluten-free carbs to have with them if they're going to be on the menu that day.

But it isn't all just about eating *before* the game. A player has to sustain himself for the entire game — neither his body nor his brain can drag — so eating *during* the game is important. An athlete needs carbs for energy, because during the game she's pulling energy from all of her muscles in order to perform and the nutrients need to keep flowing. This is just common sense, though most players will drink only something like Gatorade during the game; for me, feeding time is at least every two hours. I bring my own shake to drink on the sidelines, and it is filled with protein, carbs, and amino acids. Importantly, I don't just drink a shake during the games, but during workouts at the gym as well. I want every workout to count. I'm putting my all into agility and conditioning drills, or lifting weights, and I need to keep the nutrients flowing then, too.

After the game? Ask any kid who's ever played any sport at all: you are ravenous when you walk off the field! That's when you want a feast of lean protein, gluten-free pasta, and vegetables in every color of the rainbow. In youth sports, however — and I know this from my own experience — kids are often told to go drink a glass of chocolate milk to replenish their body with the nutrients it has spent during the game, and this is just not good advice at all. You absolutely need to replenish protein and carbs, but why not a protein that's actually good for you? Why a simple carb like sugar — which will certainly get your blood sugar back up fast, but then send it crashing back down just as quickly. Sometimes I think the chocolate milk recommendation is so pervasive only because most kids will willingly drink it. But there are other foods just as yummy that are so much better for you after a game. A big bowl of gluten-free pasta prima vera with some sautéed shrimp on top. Grilled beef-and-vegetable kabobs. Even that perennial favorite, pizza, can get a pass if it's made right — and by right I mean gluten- and casein-free — and topped with lean proteins and lots of veggies.

Your food choices shouldn't change, however, even if it isn't game day. For me, I know I feel better if I stay on track, and I believe it is especially important to take care of myself during off-season. One day, when I was working out at a gym in Jacksonville, I ran into Jack Del Rio. Jack is a former NFL player and at that time was the head coach for the team that drafted me in the first round, the Jacksonville Jaguars. He asked me what I was doing working out already — the season had just ended a week prior. My answer was simply that I feel better when I work out regularly, and that's a valid point all on its own. But thinking more about it now, I realize that if I let time go by and don't take care of myself, I'll have a more difficult time when the season does start. At the end of the day, it's easier to *stay* in shape than to *get* in shape.

Now, I don't load up on food during the off-season the way I do during training, or on a game day, when I'm putting my body through that rigor. But I do keep my choices healthy, and I throw in at least one shake a day. When you're at the top of your game and you're eating right, changing your diet back to the bad stuff makes for a dramatic change. Both your body and your brain start to feel

Julie's Scrumptious Post-game Chocolate-Banana Shake

Try this as a post-game pick-me-up in place of chocolate milk—you'll feel good, and your kid will feel great!

Ingredients:

2 scoops of a good quality chocolate-flavored protein powder—a combination of rice and pea protein is my preferred source

1 cup almond milk

1 ripe banana

1 teaspoon honey

2 tablespoons nut butter (peanut, almond, or cashew)

Water as needed

Mix well in a blender and drink up!

Why these particular ingredients? Well, first of all, because you want to make it yummy for kids so they'll think of their nutritious shakes as treats. And who among us doesn't like a good chocolate and banana combo? But there are other reasons you want all of these goodies in your after-game shake.

You want *protein powder* to help them rebuild the muscles they've been using so hard in the game. There are a lot of different protein powders on the market these days and most of them are chalky—kids aren't going to like their taste. In any case, you have to read the label to determine what kind of protein is inside the package. You definitely want to stay away from soy-based proteins. My current favorite is a brand called Orgain, an organic, gluten- and casein-free, plant-based protein powder made with sprouted brown rice, chia, hemp, and pea proteins, that provides twenty-one full grams of protein in each serving, which is two scoops. This brand also contains thirteen grams of carbohydrates in each scoop and, after a game, it's important for athletes to replace the carbs they've just burned during play. Those carbs will often make it a no-no for professional athletes, but for growing youth, it's not necessarily bad, and that extra carbohydrate makes it one of the most palatable to drink with just water that I have ever tasted.

I'm not an advocate of feeding children animal milk (see Eugene's note on the essential book, *Don't Drink Your Milk*), so I recommend *almond milk* as a substitute. It has a lovely nutty flavor, contains no cholesterol or lactic acids, and is rich with the nutrients kids need like fiber, Vitamin E, magnesium, and calcium. Further, it contains prebiotic properties that help maintain a healthy level of good bacteria in the digestive tract.

The *banana* gives the drink another layer of flavor as well as the creamy texture kids expect in their shakes. Additionally, a banana provides the body with fiber, carbs, protein, and other nutrients like Vitamin A, Vitamin B6, folic acid, thiamine, niacin, and riboflavin.

Nut butter is an easy way to get some healthy fat into your kid's diet—and your kid needs healthy fat for so many reasons. Admittedly, peanuts are legumes, not nuts, but they are generally widely accepted by kids and are a great starting point for adding fat to a shake. *Myelin*, the fatty layer that wraps around and protects the cells in our neural network so they can fire off the electrical messages that allow us to think, speak, and move with speed and clarity, is made from fat. For our purposes here, you know that when your kid gets off the playing field, he is going to be really hungry, more than ready to replace all the energy he has just burned, and healthy fat is what is going to profoundly satisfy this hunger, and keep him from being hungry again in twenty minutes.

You can also add a few special ingredients to your shake to make it an even more powerful tool for your child's recovery from his workout. *D-ribose,* in a dose of about 5000 mg is a healthy sugar that very specifically helps muscles to recover faster after a workout. *Carnitine tartrate*, helps muscles recover, too, but it also boosts the function of the mitochondria—the "power plants" inside each and every cell of the body that manufacture the cell's energy. His cells have just been working overtime, allowing him to play his sport, and giving his mito-chondria a little extra nutrition as he cools down helps to protect them. Working up to a dose of about 30mg/kg or 12mg/pound of body weight is safe. If your child doesn't metabolize it well, he may start to smell "fishy" and I always stop it if that happens. You can also add *n-ace-tyl-cysteine*, or *NAC*, at a dose of up to 900 mg, which has amazing anti-oxidant properties and is a precursor to glutathione, the body's own master anti-oxidant. NAC also does one more thing: it helps to heal torn muscle tissue, so it eases any muscle aches, and makes it easier for your kid to go back and do it all again the next day without feeling sore. We'll cover how to make sure you're buying good quality supple-ments in the next section of this book—supplements aren't helpful if they aren't quality.

sluggish. I eat healthily consistently because I don't like the toll that garbage food takes on me. Try this experiment: eat only healthy foods for one solid week, then take a day off; you'll feel the slump by noon.

This doesn't mean that everyone has to eat pristinely all the time. We personally never relent on the gluten- and casein-free portion of our approach to food, and I know Julie feels very strongly about that as well, especially for her individuals with autism, but it is OK to indulge once in a while — go ahead and order in a pizza on family movie night, or let your kid have an ice cream cone when she's out with friends. Just help her to not make a habit of eating the bad stuff — once in a while is not once a week. It's shocking how easy it is for that indulgence to go from once in a blue moon to becoming once a month, to once a week, to once a day — it's why I choose to be so very disciplined in my approach. Trying to navigate that slippery slope is likely to land you right on your behind!

There is one indulgence, however, that I feel obligated to talk about here, and that's drinking, particularly for college-aged readers and their parents. If you're in college, you're probably drinking. I know I drank in college; in some ways, in our contemporary culture, the kegger at the frat house is almost a rite of passage. And, I suppose, if you're of age, and, importantly, if you don't have to drive after having a drink, a couple of beers isn't going to hurt you. You're young enough at that age for your body to recover, and relatively quickly, from this indulgence. But if you're drinking until you're stupid — and/or, worse, drinking *regularly* until you're stupid — you're putting your body through real trauma. And if you're a college-level athlete who's drinking heavily, you will likely never reach the potential you might have attained in your sport if you either drank moderately, or didn't drink at all. If you don't put the right stuff in, or *if you put too much of the wrong stuff in*, you won't get the performance out. Plain as that.

 " Eating well is simple, but it can be scary for folks who have never done it before. "

When I was pregnant, I was hyper-aware that I was eating for two, and, as a consequence, very aware of what I put in my mouth. I was a practicing, traditional pediatrician back then, but I don't think that gave me terribly special insight into the link between pregnancy and proper nutrition. Like almost all soon-to-be-moms, I was careful about every morsel, because I knew that the nutrients I was providing to my body were what were going to impact the development of the child I was carrying.

Here's the question, then: do any of us really believe that wholesome, nutrient-dense foods are any less important to the critical developmental stages of infancy, toddlerhood, early childhood, the tween or the teenage years than they are to fetal development? No, right? OK, so think about this: our Little Leaguers, and soccer and basketball players, and swimmers and budding tennis pros and track stars and wrestlers need fuel not only to grow, but to have the stamina to compete. So, how do we keep our active kids — and it is a rare kid, indeed, who isn't active in some way — eating these wholesome, nutrient-dense foods once they're actually out of our bodies?

Taste. Moms and dads want their kids' food to be nutritious; kids need food to be tasty and yummy and lip-smacking. Big order? Let me tell you a little story about my go-to source, Chef Rebecca Katz.[1] The first time I saw Chef Katz cook, she was giving a demonstration. She started by offering her audience a taste of what we'd all consider a standard, healthy, if hum-drum meal. We all bit and chewed and swallowed, and shrugged. Our kids would never go for what was on that plate. But, *wait!* She went back behind her kitchen set-up and made the same meal, only this time she added some herbs, a few dashes of citrus zest, salt, and even some squirts of fresh fruit juices here and there and — one more taste and I was an immediate convert. The food was still healthy, but now it was fabulously delicious! And my family? They were over the moon about the food I had learned to prepare for them. There

---

1 http://rebeccakatz.com.

are other chefs and cooks I rely on for recipes and tricks to make meals into real treats — you'll find a list in the Resource section of this book, including one of my favorites, Jessica Seinfeld's classic, *Deceptively Delicious: Simple Secrets to Get Your Kids Eating Good Food.*[2] But for a one-stop-shop you are going to want to visit (and revisit and revisit) Chef's Katz's web site.

The other part of making sure your family is getting as much nutrition as possible from the foods they eat is to buy organic ingredients. Now, I know buying organic can be more costly than ingredients produced by big agriculture, so let me amend this recommendation and hammer home once again the advice to buy as many organic ingredients as the family budget will allow, and be sure to focus on that dirty dozen list of most contaminated foods.[3]

But, that said, let's talk a little bit about cost versus value, and how that relates to organic foods. First of all, if you count it as a benefit that your food tastes good, organic will win hands down over the fresh-from-the-refrigerated-truck stuff any day. But if you count value as the quality of the food, the dollars you lay out on organic products are even better spent. Pound for pound, because organic produce is grown without pesticides, using more land- and people-friendly farming practices, you are going to get more Vitamin C and essential minerals, and fewer nitrates and heavy metals than in factory- farm fruits and vegetables. Because livestock that are raised organically are better fed, better exercised, and have fewer health problems than conventionally farmed animals, organic meats are leaner, contain fewer or no antibiotics, and are free of the sort of

2 http://www.amazon.com/Deceptively-Delicious-Simple-Secrets-Eating/dp/006176793X.
3 http://www.ewg.org/foodnews

The Dirty Dozen

Getting your kids to eat vitamin- and antioxidant-packed fruits and vegetables can be a real challenge for a parent—and affording organically grown produce can be a real challenge to the family budget. Believe me, I know this first-hand. But, here's the thing: in a world where the bulk of the food we can buy at the average grocery store is grown by big-agriculture, we can pretty much assume that most of it has been heavily sprayed with pesticides. That said, there are some fruits and veggies that are more susceptible to insect and fungus infestation and are therefore more heavily sprayed with toxins than others—these are the ones that you *always* want to buy in their organic forms. Here's a list of the current top twelve—you can check for changes at www.ewg.org/foodnews/.

Apples. Because so many different insects and kinds of fungus threaten apple harvests, this is one of the most heavily sprayed crops in the world. More than forty different pesticides are used to combat these threats and, not coincidentally, traces of these pesticides can also be found in commercially produced applesauce, apple juice, and other apple products. If organic apples aren't available to you—and even considering that apple rinds are rich in nutrients—we recommend that you peel them before eating.

Bell peppers. In every sweet, antioxidant color they come in, they can come laced with over fifty different pesticides. There is no substitute, so go organic with this fruit.

Celery. USDA tests have detected over sixty different pesticides on celery samples. If you can't find organic celery, try radishes or kohlrabi for a nice, crisp raw crunch.

Potatoes. The lowly potato—and the French fries and chips and Thanksgiving side dish of mashed that are made from it: over thirty-five different pesticides are used on this crop. For fresh, try substituting sweet potatoes and yams if you can't find organic. As for processed foods—those sometimes-irresistible fast-food fries included—this pesticide contamination is one more reason you're better off resisting your kid's pleas for a drive-thru snack.

Spinach. Fifty different pesticides have been detected in both fresh and frozen spinach, and the canned variety doesn't fare much better. Popeye would weep. This is a must-buy-organic vegetable.

Lettuce. Right up there with spinach and its fifty different pesticides. If you can't find organic, it is better to forego the salad and go with greens like broccoli, green beans, or asparagus.

Kale. For a leafy green—and a particularly hardy one to boot—it is almost as contaminated as spinach and lettuce. Try Swiss chard instead if you can't find organic.

Strawberries. Strawberries are especially susceptible to fungus and, in turn, big-agriculture sprays them heavily to keep their crops "healthy." Substitute pineapples, bananas, and kiwis if you can't find organic.

Blueberries. And cranberries and cherries. While the latter two often contain less than the fifty different pesticides that are used on blueberries, they are often just as contaminated.

Peaches. Fresh, juicy, delicious peaches! It's almost a crime that over sixty pesticides have been found on this scrumptious fruit! But if you can't find organic, we recommend you substitute a different fruit, or try using canned peaches as they tend to contain less pesticides than the fresh, non-organic fruit.

Nectarines. Imported nectarines are one of the most highly contaminated fruits you'll find in your grocer's produce section. Domestically grown ones fare much better, but we'd still recommend substituting if you can't find organic. Pineapples and mangos are a better choice.

Grapes. Over thirty different pesticides have been detected on grapes of all varieties. Ditto the raisins that are made from the grapes. And, you won't be stunned to find out, in the wine that is also made from them. They are so contaminated as a crop that we recommend only organic grapes and grape products.

infectious agents that have been linked to things like mad cow disease.[1]

There are certain items that all of us splurge on because we appreciate the superiority of the product. I'll spend a few dollars more on a bottle of brand-name toenail polish because it covers better than the same color of the drugstore brand. My husband insists on buying the more expensive grade of gas because the car runs more smoothly on the better grade. I urge you to consider how much more smoothly your body will run — and how much better you will feel — when you start feeding it a better grade of food.

POOP, PLAIN AND SIMPLE

So, we've all heard that old truism: what goes up, must come down. Throw a baseball in the air and, sooner or later, it falls back down to earth — even if it comes down over the fence and in the neighbor's yard, crashes through your family room window, or lands on the roof. Gravity; the descent is inevitable.

The same is true with food and poop: if you eat something — be it healthy and clean real food or junk food, a chicken and broccoli and carrot stir-fry or a greasy fast "food" burger and the cardboard fries that almost inescapably accompany it — it is eventually going to reemerge from your body in the form of poop. The form the poop takes when it leaves your body, and the ease and/or difficulty of the evacuation, however, are extremely good indicators of the sort of food you're eating, and how well your body is using what you're feeding it.

To help my patients understand how important this poop thing is, I introduce the topic by playing a game. The

---

1 http://www.organic.org/articles/showarticle/article-46.

premise is that they are going to be taken to my home, blind-folded, and allowed to choose ONE thing to be looking at when the blind-fold comes off. Whatever they choose to look at, they need to learn, *from that one thing they're looking at*, as much as possible about my family and me. They'll pick the living room, the computer room, and occasionally a mom will guess the fridge — and then I tell them I choose the kitchen trash. The junk mail goes there, so I'll know names, interests, and what the marketing data thinks their income is. School papers go there, so I'll know names, ages, schools, teachers, grades and other academic strengths and weaknesses. I'll know if there's a pet, what the pet eats and/or refuses, whether or not they recycle, whether or not they compost, whether they cook or order in, whether or not the kids eat what is prepared for them, and how organic they choose to be. All from the trash can.

So, thinking along analogous terms, if I want to learn as much as possible about the human body in front of me, I need to learn about the body's equivalent of the kitchen trash — poop.

I warned you earlier in this book that no one — including most physicians — pays nearly enough attention to poop and that we were going to correct that in these pages. So here goes.

The Bristol Stool Scale, sometimes also known as the Bristol Stool Chart as well as the Meyers Chart, is a medical tool that helps doctors to assess the health of the human colon by classifying the different types of poop we humans produce. It was created at the University of Bristol, a research university in the United Kingdom, by Dr. Ken Heaton and first published in 1997. While it has its limits as a diagnostic tool, it remains a great way to establish a baseline for talking about bowel health with patients. Dr.

THE BRISTOL POOP CHART

Pick a name!	What's it look like?	Description	A.K.A.
Shape 1		Separate hard balls or lumps, hard to pass, spends too much time in colon.	Kix, Milk Duds, goat pellts, Bristol balls (or bullets)
Shape 2		Lumpy fecal balls stuck together, can produce hemorrhoids.	Monkey bread. The Little General.
Shape 3		Like a sausage with cracks on the surface, mild straining, low end of acceptable.	Cracked sausage, pine cone, corn on the cob.
Shape 4		Like a banana, snake, can be 'S'-shaped; soft and moist, not too hard, not too soft—juuust right!	Goldilocks Poop, Top Banana, tame dolphin, The Champ.
Shape 5		Soft blobs, clear-cut edges, passes easily, high end of acceptable, typical of several stools per day.	Bristol blobs, happy travelers, soggy chicken nuggets
Shape 6		Ragged edges, mushy stool, ribbon shapes, requires excess wiping. Could be a sign of stress or IBS.	Fluffy poop, porridge
Shape 7		Diarrhea. Not good.	Fountain of Poop, gravy, the Unfortunate Squirts

Heaton categorized seven different types of human poop, ranging from the sorts you're likely to see from patients who are constipated to those who are complaining of diarrhea.

Type 1 is poop that presents as separate, hard lumps, rather like nuts, that are difficult to pass.

Type 2 is a sausage-shaped poop that is hard and lumpy, as if it is made up of those separate, nut-like lumps clinging together. Type 2 may be slightly easier to pass, but both Type 1 and Type 2 indicate that the patient is likely experiencing constipation.

Type 3 also presents as a sausage-like poop, but instead of looking as if it is made up of separate lumps, it merely has cracks in its surface; it is indicative of a fairly healthy bowel — producing stool that has a sufficient amount of moisture and, thus, a patient who can have a bowel movement without straining.

Type 4 is the gold standard of poop — it looks like a sausage, or a snake; its surface is smooth and its consistency is soft, like peanut butter.

Type 5 presents as soft blobs but with clearly defined edges.

Type 6 is a mushy stool made up of "fluffy" pieces with ragged edges.

Type 7 is a watery stool that contains no solid pieces — it is entirely liquid. These last three types indicate the patient is suffering from diarrhea.

Are there other things to look for in poop to help you assess your health and that of your child? Indeed. Are there parts of undigested food in the poop? If so, it could indicate either that your kiddo doesn't have the enzymes or probiotic bacteria she needs, or that he has insufficient acids in his gut to breakdown the food. Try adding the juice of half a lemon to his morning juice or juice drink to increase the acid level. Or add some fermented foods to her diet, like sauerkraut, pickles, or casein-free yogurt — my family loves coconut yogurt best. Or try some freshly made juice, which has enzymes present for about twenty minutes directly after juicing that are amazingly powerful. The other two things that you may see in poop are mucus and blood. Neither of these are normal, and warrant a conversation with your child's doctor if they occur.

Next, how often does your child evacuate his bowels? The standard is to poop two to three times a day — really! But if he's pooping only two to three times a week, that means that feces is backing up and being stored in his body — allowing the body to reabsorb the toxins that it was trying to dispose of by way of the excrement. More water, along with more fiber in his diet, is going to help correct this problem. Does the smell of the poop make the bathroom unusable by any other family member until you call in the HAZMAT team — or make the other kids on his team tease him when he has to use the locker room to have at it? Poop isn't something you'd ever mistake for potpourri, of course, but the smell of a healthy poop is something easily controlled by being submerged in toilet water and flushed away. There are all sorts of products on the market — aerosols and spritzers and even oils that can mask the odor of your stool so others experience no nasal discomfort after you've used the powder room — but all they make me think about is that the people who use them are masking serious bowel and colon issues with perfumes and need to go to see a doctor rather than pick up another air spray at the supermarket. And what about "floaters" — poop that doesn't sink into the toilet water but floats near the surface? Well, floaters can actually be desirable! Floating poop indicates that your kid has a healthy level of fiber and fatty acids in his diet. However, floaters can also occur when there's way too much fat in the poop, so we have to consider floaters in the context of the diet of the person making them.

So, how can you get your kid on the gold standard? A colorful diet with plenty of water, high in fiber and living foods, and low in processed foods, plain and simple. I know it's tradition to take the team out to the favorite local pizza joint to celebrate if they've won the game, or console them if they haven't, but any nutrition they get from a standard American pizza isn't going to help their bodies recover from the energy they've just expended in play — and you will, eventually, be able to read the results of repeated pizza fests in what ends up in the toilet bowl. If you put garbage food in your mouth, you're going to end up with garbage coming out. How great would it be for our kids if we parents all banded together and started a tradition of protein-packed, fresh fruit-and-veggie smoothie parties after the games? I know the kids would think we were a little nuts, at first, but my bet is that they'd feel so much better immediately — and be able to play so much harder the next day — that, after a while, they'd be all-in, too!

HORMONES, PUBERTY... AND CARBS

Youth sports teams are organized by our kids' ages or grades in school. Seven-year-olds don't play baseball with fourteen-year-olds; middle school kids play on middle school football teams and high school kids work toward playing in the varsity lineup. This way of organization has less to do with age, per se, than with our kids' relative size and development at those ages. The pre-pubescent body is

Sugar Addiction

I thought that a section about hormones and carbs was a good place to pause for a quick aside about how sugar and high-glycemic white food carbs light up a particular part of our brains—the *nucleus accumbens*.

The nucleus accumbens is located in the region of the brain called the basal forebrain and, while we humans use this part of our brain for a variety of functions, its most significant role is as our hedonistic pleasure center. It is the place in your brain where you process motivation, reward, and reinforcement—and regulate your behaviors relative to pleasures such as food, exercise and sex, as well as drugs such as alcohol, nicotine, cannabis, cocaine, and opiates. It has been said by recovering drug addicts that "Cocaine makes you feel like a new man—and the first thing the new man wants is more cocaine." This is because, when a person uses cocaine, the drug causes the nucleus accumbens to light up like the proverbial Christmas tree, sending the message "Wow! This is fun! Give me more, more, more!" because *it wants to stay lit up*.

Well, this pleasure center lights up when a person ingests sugar in the same way it lights up when a person uses cocaine.[1] It sends the same message—"More, more, more!" because it wants to stay lit up.

The problem is that we humans develop tolerance to the substances that activate the nucleus accumbens; we start to need greater and greater quantities of the drug—cocaine or sugar, for example—that triggers our pleasure center.

And that is how addiction begins.

Is your kid addicted to carbs? What does he ask for when he requests a snack? What does she want to order when your family goes out to eat? What comes back uneaten in his school lunch box? If the answers are cupcakes, ice cream, pasta, bread, and, for that last question, carrot sticks, you may have to think about helping to wean your kiddos off their sugar highs and getting them onto enjoying more veggies and proteins.

---

1 https://www.psychologytoday.com/blog/eating-mindfully/201204/sugar-addiction.

much different than the pubescent and post-pubescent one, and sending a team of seventh graders onto a basketball court with a team of twelfth graders would be asking those kids to compete on a playing field that was not only unlevel, but unsafe.

For us parents, it's really a no-brainer that our kids should compete with kids their own size. What we might not know, however, is that we have one more dietary trick that can help our kids through the tough transition of puberty — keep them moving more painlessly, both physically and emotionally, through the turmoil of adolescent growth.

Puberty is triggered by a drop in *gaba*. Gaba, or gamma-aminobutyric acid, is a biochemical that's made in our brains and when the level that your child's body is manufacturing drops, you will likely know it as the drop is often accompanied by an increase in anxiety and irritability — or what we commonly write off as typical teenage moodiness or surliness. What can exacerbate this irritability and anxiety we see as puberty is something I have termed CCC — Chronic Carb Consumption.

Kids love carbs — pizza and ice cream and all of that bready, sugary stuff — and we make it easy for them to get all the stuff they love. About 70% of the food in the Standard American Diet (SAD) is processed,[1] and processed foods are wicked with added sugars![2]

What happens to chronic carb consumers is that they have chronically elevated levels of insulin as their bodies try to cope with all that sugar in the SAD. When insulin is chronically high, sex hormone binding globulin (SHBG) falls. SHBG does exactly what it says it does. It binds sex

---

1 http://www.marketplace.org/topics/life/big-book/processed-foods-make-70-percent-us-diet.
2 http://www.hsph.harvard.edu/nutritionsource/carbohydrates/added-sugar-in-the-diet/.

The Power of Juice!

Juicing—it's one of the best tricks I know for getting vitamins, minerals, and *enzymes* into kids.

Enzymes are naturally-occurring proteins that stimulate, and even improve upon or accelerate, the body's biological functions. There are *digestive enzymes* that break foods down so their nutrients can be absorbed more effectively by the body, and *metabolic enzymes* that help to build new cells and repair damaged ones. Fresh juice is alive with both kinds—but only for about twenty minutes after the juice is extracted from the fruit or vegetable, so juicing at home, minutes before you consume the goodness, is key.

A good juicer has become a standard small appliance in my kitchen; I use a Green Star Twin Gear model—a sturdy and reliable, if slightly pricey, machine. I like it because it uses flat surfaces to *triturate*, or press, the foods to extract the juice, rather than using blades, so there's a *lot* less waste. Yes, it does unfortunately remove some of the fiber from the foods, but as a trade off with palatability, it is worth it.

There is more than just one machine that can serve the purpose of a juicer, certainly. Many of you might think a plain old blender would do the job, but a blender won't rupture the cells of the fruits and vegetables—releasing their enzymes so the body can most easily absorb them. To rupture the cells you need a juicer, or a Vitamix. As a less expensive alternative to the Vitamix, you might want to try the NutriBullet[1]. With both the Vitamix and the NutriBullet, all the fiber stays in the drink, so there is no waste whatsoever. While I prefer the smooth texture of the drink I get from my Green Star juicer, some people prefer the thicker and creamier, more shake-like product that results from a Vitamix or Vitamix-like machine. In short, if immediate cost is the main factor, choose a NutriBullet. If your concern is texture, go with the Green Star, and if its about the diversity of functions the machine can handle,

---

1 https://www.nutribullet.com.

go with the Vitamix, which is incredibly handy in the kitchen for making soups and sauces as well as your morning beverage.

I can't emphasize enough the importance of using organic fruits and vegetables for juicing—who wants petrochemical residues mixed in with such a life-giving cocktail? I am also a huge proponent of juicing *green stuff*—kale, spinach, Swiss chard. In short, veggies that are loaded with iron! I am a survivor of breast cancer and, during treatment, I shocked my oncologist by getting my iron level from 7.2 to 10 just two weeks after my surgery—not by taking iron supplements, but by juicing boatloads of green stuff and drinking a luscious sixteen-ounce glass of it every morning.

Here's a recipe for a simple, homemade, nutrient-packed juice your kids will love:

Two heaping handfuls of fresh spinach
One tart apple
One large orange
One stalk crisp celery
Two large carrots
One medium tomato
Half an avocado

Put it all through your juicer, or mix it up in your Vitamix or NutriBullet, and let your kids enjoy the yumminess—but don't let them enjoy it alone because it is good for you, too! For a little twist, run a sprig of mint through the juicer—I love its flavor in my morning green drink.

hormones so that they are neutralized, ready to be active when needed, not just raging around the body freely wreaking havoc. So when SHBG falls, as you can well imagine, the sex hormones — estrogen and, particularly testosterone — will rise too high and get out of balance.

And these levels increase for girls as well as boys.

And what do increased hormone levels lead to? Early puberty, increased aggression in both sexes, decreased flexibility — which can translate to easier injury — and irregular and painful menstrual cycles for girls.

Hormones govern so much of our children's growth and behaviors, changing their bodies and brains in ways that are incredibly disruptive to what they have always, prior to the onset puberty, known about themselves and the world around them. It costs the body an enormous amount of energy to grow — give your kids an extra edge by helping them to cut out unhealthy carbs, especially at this fragile stage of development.

SUPPLEMENTS

You may well think that getting kids to eat a better grade of food — and on a consistent basis — is an uphill battle. You know the importance of providing your child with nutritious food; you know that his entire physical development, not just his ability to play a sport well, depends on his body having the right ingredients to grow and mature. We've already dived into brain health, and how the brain works and uses nutrients, but all of us parents know, in a way that goes well beyond intuition, that we have to nourish our children's brains so they can reach their full mental development. A brain deprived of proper nutrients and a brain that is fully nourished are wholly different things in terms of learning, performing, and even emotional maturity and stability — as different as a three-wheeled carriage drawn by an ancient mare is from a Formula One sports car primed for a Grand Prix.

Getting kids to buy into all of this — that can be the hard part.

But loading them up with the vitamins, minerals, proteins, carbs, and other nutrients their bodies crave need not be the sort of "food fight" every parent dreads. How? First things first: organic, organic, organic — as much as the family budget will allow. If you use as many organic ingredients as you can, you will automatically be giving your kids superior nutrition because, as we have already discussed, organic produce and other foods contain higher concentrations of nutrients.

Most supermarkets have sections where they feature, at the very least, organic produce and meats. Farmer's markets are also a good bet for procuring part of your weekly grocery order. Keep in mind that many farmers, though they adhere to standards of organic-farming practice, are not *certified* organic. *Organic* is a legal designation and, as such, comes with requirements that some small farmers haven't had time or other resources to fulfill. Ask the farmer unloading his truck how his produce is grown or his cattle have been raised and you will most often hear that no petrochemicals or antibiotics have been used to raise the foods he is selling — and you may even get an invitation to come visit the farm to see for yourself! These assurances from the source are fair enough for me to often feel comfortable serving my family their products. And, once you have converted your young children to the goodness of whole, organic foods, take heart — farmer's markets are springing up on college campuses, responding to the demand of our college-aged kiddos for hearty, wholesome nourishment that goes beyond what a lot of college cafeterias still offer. In recent months, I actually have been encouraged, even thrilled, to see teens and young adults choosing to sit around at healthy food markets — like Native Sun here in Jacksonville, or Whole Foods, EarthFare, and Trader Joe's — studying and

Kids as Chefs—and Gardeners, too!

In our house, the kitchen and the garden are two of the kids' favorite places—my husband and I started to teach them basic cooking and gardening skills as soon as they were old enough to stand on a step-stool to reach the sink or wield a child-sized hoe. Here are my top five reasons why I think every child should have the advantages of knowing how to both plant a garden and get around in a kitchen.

1. There are no better venues for teaching a child about nutrition. The vibrant color of a carrot pulled from the ground, the aromas of the herb garden, the flavor of a still warm, sun-ripened tomato! These are the tastes and sensations around which lessons about nutrition are most delicious—and best absorbed.

2. These are skill sets that will serve them all their lives. Let's face it: the odds of any of our children ending up with a full-time chef on the staff are pretty long. Learning to prepare good, whole food for himself will go a long way toward saving him from the fast "food" fall-back position when he strikes out in the world on his own.

3. There is a great sense of pride and accomplishment for any child when the whole family enjoys the lettuce she grew in the backyard or the dinner he cooked himself.

having a snack rather than wandering the mall with a pack of French fries in their hands.

In addition to a healthy diet, you can augment your child's routine with dietary supplements. Supplements provide a way to make sure your kids are getting a full complement of nutrients on a daily basis, even if they balk at a serving of squash, or refuse the fish you've so carefully prepared.

So, what supplements should your child be taking? Well, I'm not your child's doctor so I haven't drawn blood, asked

4. In a busy, two-career household, there are many days when the time it takes to prepare dinner is also the only real family time that fits in a twenty-four-hour period. Instead of Dad reading the paper and the kids killing time with video games while Mom throws something together alone in the kitchen for everyone to eat, why not make cooking together a time for family fun and bonding!

5. Picky eaters are more likely to eat foods *they have prepared themselves*. Enough said.

Wait! Bonus Reason!

Growing a garden and following a recipe are great ways to help your kids with their math! For example, when Matthew was younger and studying multiplication, I often doubled a recipe for soup or a chicken dish that I knew would keep and work well for leftovers, and I'd ask him to calculate what we'd need at the grocery store to gather all the ingredients to make twice as much. When he got a little older, I asked him to measure the area and depth of the new raised beds in our backyard and calculate the amount of topsoil we'd need to purchase. These activities offer all sorts of opportunities to reinforce in very practical ways the lessons they're learning in the classroom.

about poop, enquired about the family approach to nutrition and done a full analysis of what your child should be getting more of, but I can offer general guidelines to help you make good choices.

First, because the profound sort of physical output a young athlete experiences depletes the protein her body needs to grow and function, supplementing protein intake with a good protein powder is probably key. I recommend staying away from whey-based protein powders; indeed, the brand you choose should be casein-free — that is, should not contain any milk products. This often results in using plant-based proteins, and a combination of pea and rice protein provides the complete spectrum of amino acids.

Next, because intense physical exercise can stress the adrenal glands, you might provide your child with a good B complex supplement to support her adrenals.

For the improvement of your child's overall health, I recommend adding Vitamin D3 to most diets at a dose of between 1000 and 5000 units per day. We human beings were designed to spend almost all our daylight hours outdoors and naked, getting our necessary dose of Vitamin D from the sun — but these are activities and customs that have gone out of fashion in the thousands of years that have intervened between our earliest ancestors and us. What this means, however, this radical change in our clothes-wearing, spending-time-outside habits, is that even those of us who enjoy regular outdoor activities are likely not getting as much Vitamin D-filled sunshine as we truly require. Keep in mind that while there is no upper limit on the amount of Vitamin D our bodies can handle over short intervals, Vitamin D does absolutely impact calcium metabolism and gross overuse of Vitamin D3 for months on end does have the potential to raise calcium levels in the blood too high. I recommend that you have a doctor draw your blood/your kid's blood and do an analysis of it. Most practitioners of functional medicine are looking for a level of between 60 and 80 iu/ml blood for optimum function of calcium regulation, immune system, serotonin levels, and even steroid hormone regulation. Some people manage to function with levels as low as eight or ten and many run around with levels just barely in range in the low 30s. As Vitamin D is a precursor to serotonin, are we really then surprised that so many folks go about feeling sluggish, tired, and even depressed?

Carnitine tartrate, which comes in powder form, should potentially be a part of your supplement routine — it is dosed by weight, so look carefully at the labeling. Add the recommended amount to your athlete's protein shake — to support and protect her mitochondria. Here's a little pearl of wisdom: if your athlete's sweat starts to smell "fishy", she may be having trouble metabolizing the carnitine, and you will need to back down on the dose. Or consider trying a different form of carnitine. There are many available, and, as you can imagine, the variety is accompanied by a great deal of discussion among health care professionals about what the best form is. In actuality, the best form of carnitine is the one to which your athlete responds best.

I often recommend Vitamin C, a great anti-oxidant, for kids, too, though most kids are pretty fond of citrus fruits and juices. If your kid is a fan of citrus, drinking at least one glass of citrus juice *without added sugar* and/or munching down at least two citrus fruits a day, you can probably offer the Vitamin C only when you see that he is under stress, or feeling rundown.

Finally, you should consider adding fish oil, rich in Omega-3s, to your child's supplement routine as well. Healthy fatty acids like Omega-3s are deficient in the Standard American Diet (SAD); adding up to 4000 mg a day, depending on the size of your athlete, as a supplement will give her a good supply. If you and your family follow a vegan diet, substitute flax oils for fish oil. I love to add flax meal or chia seeds to our veggies and salads — not only do I add omegas that way, but I sneak in more fiber in a palatable way. To avoid the blood thinning tendencies of omegas, be sure to be taking in enough balancing Vitamin

K by eating those delicious dark green leafy veggies like kale and spinach. It's important to note here that as much as I hate doing it, when my athletes are "hitting", I have them decrease the omegas so as to avoid any potential for increased bruising. In the off-season, though, we increase it again and try to make up for lost time.

I THINK IT is important to pause here and talk about the quality of the supplements you're giving to your child, because quality of supplements really, really matters.

Let's talk fish oil for a second. I most often recommend my patients purchase their fish oil supplements from a company called Nordic Naturals. Why? Well, first of all because I know how the company produces its supplements — I've taken a tour of their pristine manufacturing facility. Part of their process — and they are one of the few companies that do this — is to remove the organs from the fish before they press them to extract their oils. And why is this so important? Water pollution. Depending on where they travel in their lifetimes, fish can swim in a real stew of toxic sludge. The heavy metals and other pollutants they ingest end up residing in the organs of their bodies — as they do for all living creatures. Removing the organs before a fish is pressed for its oils is a step that assures you won't be getting a vitamin filled not only with healthy fish oil but deadly toxic chemicals.

Second, I know about their distribution policies and practices. Their supplements, for example, have expiration dates — they haven't been sitting around in the warehouse of a big-box store for months, turning rancid and becoming so oxidized as a result that taking them might be worse for your health than taking no supplement at all.

I have made note of some of the brands of supplements I recommend in the Resources section of this book. Please keep in mind, as I state in my Author's Note, that neither my practice, nor my foundation, nor myself, personally, have any financial relationships at all with any of the companies or products I recommend — and we never will. It is simply not an ethical practice for a physician. That said, the brands I do recommend meet the requirements I need them to meet in order to feel good about giving them to my own patients and family members. You may discover other brands you'd like to try, so here's a summary of how to shop smart for supplements.

1. Check to see how many *milligrams* or *IUs* of the vitamin or other compound you're getting with each dose. Then compare *the cost per milligram or IU*. You might find that the smaller bottle with the higher price tag is actually a bargain when you compare the amount of actual vitamins in the bottle. I cannot overstate the importance of this step, folks. You pay for your supplements by weight, by unit. Be sure to calculate how many organisms of probiotics are in the bottle, how much vitamin B6 is in the entire bottle; creative labeling can confuse you. Ten billion probiotics per capsule is a lot less, and will be a lot cheaper, than seventy-five billion organisms per capsule. If your goal is to consume a hundred and fifty billion organisms daily, that ten billion organisms per capsule brand isn't so cost effective any more.

2. Check out the company that's manufactured the brand and be very careful about "proprietary"

blends — companies that keep secrets from the consumer usually have a good reason to do so. When a company keeps secrets — makes claims it can't quantify, or won't tell the consumer how much of an ingredient is in the unit they are purchasing — it's often because they fear being compared unfavorably to their competitors.

3. Find out if the company does one thing well, or if it is a giant supplement conglomerate. Nordic Naturals does fish oil well, and that's pretty much all they do. The same with the companies that manufacture some of the probiotics I like best — Klaire, and Custom Probiotics. Giant conglomerates are more likely to have looser quality standards than a company that wants to be known for making one type of product that is the best of its kind. Is your supplement produced and packaged in a controlled environment? If not, it may be oxidized by the time it gets to the retail shelf and not worth even the cheapest price. Additionally, the giants are more likely to have looser distribution standards as well, with masses of product sitting in mall or big-box warehouses, spoiling before consumers can get to them.

4. Ask if the company has an educational program. Are they interested in conversations with physicians that can improve the doctor's knowledge of nutrition, as opposed to simply making claims and selling to a gullible public?

5. Look at the label to determine if the product is "clean". There shouldn't be a lot of additives, and ideally the product should be both gluten- and casein-free. Above all, look for "sugar words" — sugar, syrup, agave, etc. — because nobody needs supplements with added sugars.

6. Remember that, in the case of supplements, the old cliché that "you get what you pay for" is absolutely true. When I'm paying for my family's monthly supply of probiotics, I always remind myself that with probiotics you "pay by the bug."

The manufacture of dietary supplements is not a regulated industry. This is a good thing because it does help to keep the cost of supplements at a reasonable level. But it also leaves the door wide open for unscrupulous manufacturers who try to take in consumers by offering seemingly low prices — for low doses of products that are full of filler. Don't be their victim.

AT THE END of the day, it is best to know what nutrients your child's body is in need of before you launch your food initiative with him. This requires cooperation with your family doctor or pediatrician — but here we return to the problem that we've discussed earlier: the real lack of education about nutrition in the traditional medical community — or what can even amount to a lack of respect for the role of food in health by some physicians. You can now equate the reluctance of some doctors to elevate the role of food in health to the level it deserves to the reluctance of some doctors back in the day to come out against tobacco use. Most people think it was big news to physicians on

January 11, 1964, when then-Surgeon General Luther Terry issued his landmark report that smoking was a direct cause of things like lung cancer, heart disease, and emphysema. The truth is that doctors had been recording their observations about the negative effects of tobacco use for several hundred years before that; it just took a few centuries for their observations to make it into the mainstream. Nutrition advocates are making really great headway these days — and I firmly believe that parents are going to be some of the prime movers in dealing SAD its well-deserved deathblow.

Ideally, your doctor will get a good-food-in, good-poop-out, sleep and activity history at your child's annual well visit, with consideration for testing blood, and report back to you that your child is lacking in Vitamin D, or needs calcium, or has borderline anemia, or so forth. Then you would know exactly the sorts of foods that need to be added to her diet, or that you should step up supplements if the food group is already showing up on her plate.

But, again, as we've already said, most doctors don't do a lot of blood tests — and they are reluctant to do one even if you ask specifically for a detailed food panel. There are several reasons for this reluctance. One is that once a doctor orders tests of this sort, then he or she is responsible for managing the results. If a doctor hasn't been adequately trained in managing nutrition, he won't be comfortable assessing and then improving your child's nutritional status in great detail. Even worse, most labs don't run detailed food panels — I like to use a lab called Alletess, which typically performs a broad range of food allergen and intolerance tests for about $100 — but labs like Alletess that produce consistent, reliable results are few and far between. To get this sort of information about your child's nutritional needs — and help with meeting those nutritional needs after you know what they are, your best bet is to consult with a functional medicine practitioner. The Institute for Functional Medicine provides a "find a practitioner" page on their web site so you can locate a doctor nearest to you.[1]

GLUTATHIONE

Before we leave the subject of supplements, I want to focus for a bit on *glutathione*, an antioxidant. To review, antioxidants are the miracle "cleaning solvents" that neutralize free radicals by liberally donating their own electrons to the free radicals, thus stabilizing them. There are three primary ways to get antioxidants into your body: diet (for example, eating citrus fruits every day); dietary supplements (Vitamins C and E); and boosting production of or supplementing the body's own supply of glutathione.

I've previously described glutathione as the body's master antioxidant — something the body manufactures all by itself. But just because the body manufactures glutathione doesn't mean it always has sufficient ingredients — or *precursors* — to make enough to keep up with the demand that body is experiencing. Let me explain.

Glutathione, in biochemical lingo, is a tripeptide, meaning that it has three components — cysteine, glutamic acid, and glycine — and it comes in two forms: an oxidized form, GSSG, which I choose to remember by using the "o" and thinking "Out-of-commission"; and a reduced form, GSH, or, again using the "r" as "Ready-to-go". The GSH foils free radicals (as well as other ROS — reactive oxygen species, like peroxides) by donating its electrons to make them

---

1 https://www.functionalmedicine.org/practitioner_search.aspx?id=117.

stable. In the process of losing its electrons in this way, it is converted to GSSG. The percentage of GSH in a healthy body is about 90 to the GSSG's 10 and, indeed, the ratio of glutathione in its reduced form and its oxidized form is sometimes used to measure a patient's level of cellular toxicity, or what we have been referring to as oxidative stress.

Glutathione's purpose in the body is much easier to explain — it protects the cell — its DNA, its membranes, and its many other parts — thus helping both to heal and to prevent disease. And there is no other substance in the world that does the job better. Recently, glutathione has been used in the treatment of diseases ranging from glaucoma to alcoholism, from cancer to anemia, from Parkinson's to asthma, cystic fibrosis, and HIV. But remember, we're approaching health from a functional medicine perspective; our goal is to stay healthy so we prevent disease from occurring in the first place. Supplementing glutathione is, therefore, an excellent addition to your family's health routine. Except that it's a lot harder to do than just buying some off-the-shelf product and popping it into your mouth.

Measuring the amount of glutathione in the body is pretty darned difficult to do. Blood and urine tests are both available to take the measure, but they must be done when the body is in a fasting state, and the samples have to be shipped chilled, in dry ice, to specialty labs... You get the picture. While doctors do use these tests to assess the level of oxidative stress a person is suffering, they are by no means routine. But the reality is that most healthy people really don't need to measure. While, theoretically, it might be possible to have too much glutathione in the human system, to reduce oxidative stress too much, that would be a difficult state to achieve in our modern world. We would have to live in a perfectly organic world with no chemical pollution — the Garden of Eden! But none of us do live there — or can; the result is that human beings are now oxidatively stressed at a level that is probably significant for everyone.

There are several ways to supplement glutathione. There are glutathione patches, for example, which are worn on the skin, but they don't work the way most patches do — that is, transdermally, with a substance being absorbed through the skin. Glutathione patches are placed on acupuncture points on the body and work by reflecting infra-red light frequencies in the body. I won't discount the science out of hand — these patches are homeopathic remedies and I have seen certain homeopathic treatments work very well. But patches are by no means the most efficient way to supplement glutathione.

There *are* many forms of transdermal glutathione out there. The reality, however, is that most of the readily available lotions and creams haven't been demonstrated to do much in the way of raising glutathione levels. There are some creams made by compounding pharmacies with a prescription from your doctor, but I have found the quality to vary from pharmacy to pharmacy, so I urge caution when reaching for a form of glutathione that is supposed to go through the skin. The fact is, even using an expertly prepared transdermal compound, it's pretty hard to get this little molecule through the skin at all.

More efficient is the nebulizer method. That is, glutathione is inhaled by way of a fine mist so it enters the body by way of the lungs. This is a fairly easy delivery method, but it does require a doctor's prescription, and there is one other downside as well: it is a challenge to keep the glutathione at a constant temperature, preventing exposure to light and to oxygen so that, by the time it is inhaled, it hasn't lost its efficacy, hasn't been oxidized, and is still viable as a medicine.

I have found glutathione infusions to be the most effective methods of dispensing the supplement. This way it is delivered directly into the blood stream where it can begin its work unmolested, and immediately. The infusions are relatively painless and quick — one quick prick of a needle that patients come not to mind in relation to how good they feel after an infusion. There are many people whose lives have been changed remarkably for the better by glutathione, and they make time to come in regularly.

In my practice, each infusion for each patient is custom-made. An infusion that includes glutathione can also include, among other things, B vitamins, Vitamin C, and minerals such as magnesium, depending on what the patient needs *that day*. Remember, what the body needs on any given day, in any given circumstance, is dynamic, and functional medicine takes that into account. Is one of my patients coming down with a cold? She might get a little extra vitamin C to fight the infection. Is one of my athletes feeling especially fatigued? A little more vitamin B for energy.

So, where can you get a glutathione infusion? Well, unlike patches, infusions must be administered with the supervision of a physician. Increasingly, integrative and functional medicine physicians are experienced in using glutathione infusions. You need to be aware that they are virtually never a "covered benefit" of your health insurance policy. Go once again to the web site for The Institute for Functional Medicine and use their "Find a Practitioner" feature.[1]

---

1 https://www.functionalmedicine.org/practitioner_search.aspx?id=117.

But let's get down to brass tacks here: of all the ways to get supplemental glutathione into the human body, injections and infusions just aren't realistic for most kids. To the rescue are supplements that can enhance glutathione levels, and which are meant to be taken by mouth. Additionally, they don't require a prescription. You've got to be very careful about the brand you choose, however, as studies have shown that glutathione is not easily absorbed orally through the gastrointestinal tract. Also, when a supplement is taken orally, it has to be processed by the digestive system before it can get into the body to do its good work — gastric juices can dilute the efficacy of the supplement. There are two very different supplements — EnduraCell and Recancostat — that are widely available, and that I believe are rock solid effective at helping to boost glutathione levels. EnduraCell's broccoli sprout powder is particularly good at helping the body to make glutathione, and it also provides a wealth of other nutrients and enzymes that address a range of problems, from alleviating skin damage caused by UV rays to protecting cells from carcinogens.[2] Recancostat is blended with flavinoids and is a very palatable way to intake glutathione. If you don't have a physician helping you to use oral glutathione delivery methods, follow the directions on the package.

HYDRATION

Most of us understand almost intuitively how very important it is to our overall health to stay hydrated. What many don't know, however, is that it is so important there is even a way for doctors to measure your *body-water percentage*

---

2 http://www.hopkinsmedicine.org/news/media/releases/Broccoli_SproutDerived_Extract_Protects_Against_Ultraviolet_Radiation.

so you can know whether you have an adequate amount of water in your body makeup. Now, what that percentage is for each individual can vary greatly depending on the person's age, general physical condition, and gender. For example, adult women generally want to aim for between 45% and 60%, while men want to aim for between 50% and 65%. Fat has less water in it than muscle, so people who carry more weight than average likely have a lower body-water percentage than a leaner person. Kids have a higher body-water content than adults — babies, when they are first born, have up to a 78% body-water level!

So, how can you tell if you and your kids have a healthy body-water level? That is, apart from eating enough fruits and vegetables — foods with high water content — and simply drinking a glass of water when we're thirsty? And, especially — considering that athletes sweat a lot more than less active kids — how can we make sure that our active kids are maintaining an adequate body-water weight?

I find that you need to worry less about exactly how much water your kids are drinking or how many servings of high water-content food they're eating per pound of the child's weight than about the color of his pee. Yes, you read that right. We're back to the baseline idea of "garbage in/garbage out," and this time it has to do with the color of his pee. If your kiddo is getting enough water, he or she should be peeing pretty close to clear, colorless liquid. The yellower the pee, the more dehydrated the person, and the more he or she needs to take in more water.

Yes, there are other signs of dehydration — thirst, of course; a dry mouth feeling, which can include cracked lips and/or difficulty swallowing; feelings of fatigue, irritation, or depression; dry and/or flushed skin; headache; rapid breathing and/or dizziness; nausea; brain fog, especially difficulty concentrating; poor skin elasticity; cramps and/or a long length of time between bathroom breaks — but the color of pee is, by a long shot, the easiest, most cost effective, most practical way to tell if you are taking in enough water.

I have one caveat here. There is a difference in pee being yellow because you're dehydrated and pee being yellow because you're taking a lot of B vitamins and your body isn't using them efficiently — but the reason for the difference in color is easy to discern. Yellow pee that is the result of dehydration comes most often in shades of pastel yellows to amber — that is, a spectrum of yellows and brown-yellows. Yellow pee that is the result of too many B vitamins is bright, unmistakable, *neon* yellow. If your kid's pee looks like it could glow in the dark, you need to reassess her intake of B vitamins; if it looks like light beer, or, worse, regular old lager, she needs to drink more water.

9

EXERCISE

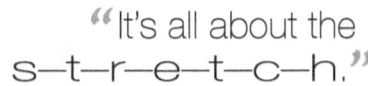
"It's all about the s—t—r—e—t—c—h."

Your kids are athletes — that's why you're reading this book. So they're already exercising! What more do we need to say about that subject?

A lot.

How your kid trains has everything to do with how he performs during a game — and, more importantly, how he maintains his health, not just during the season but all through his life.

Let me be football-specific, for a few sentences anyway, to start to illustrate some basic concepts. First of all, a football player, whether he's a pro or a college, high school, or youth league player, trains for the same thing: a series of short, explosive bursts. Each play in a football game runs for what — four seconds? There may be eighty four-second bursts of energy that a player needs to expel during the course of every game — and the player has to be able to repeat that four-second burst of energy, that four seconds of sprint/struggle/lift, efficiently each and every time he's called upon to do it, whether it's the first quarter or the fourth. I do a lot of explosive-movement work with heavy weights; I do more reps than are required in order

Bullying

Bullying is defined by the U.S. government as "unwanted, aggressive behavior among school-aged children that involves a real or perceived power imbalance. The behavior is repeated, or has the potential to be repeated, over time. Bullying includes actions such as making threats, spreading rumors, attacking someone physically or verbally, and excluding someone from a group on purpose."[1]

We agree: that about covers it. And the best policy for dealing with such behavior is *zero tolerance*. If your child is being bullied—physically bullied, cyber bullied, bullied by other children, or by a teacher or a coach—your first job is to contact the authorities in charge of the organization in question. You can visit www.stopbullying.gov for more information on prevention and appropriate response.

---

1 http://www.stopbullying.gov/what-is-bullying/index.html.

to increase my strength and build muscular endurance; and I do hours of cardio work to increase my stamina so I can make it through the grind of the grueling practices and games.

That said, an athlete trains differently for every sport in which she participates. Each activity has its own discipline — runners train differently than swimmers, who train differently than baseball players, who have different training basics than tennis players. But what every athlete has in common is that she needs to *train beyond what she will be called to do on the field of play*. If you don't strive, in your controlled training situations, to push yourself to the point of working as hard as you'll need to work when you are called upon to do it in the course of actual play, that's when injuries happen.

Training properly means striving to be stronger and/or faster than you will need to be during the next game. It means not ducking out of practice because it's raining and you don't feel like getting wet, or you're not really in the mood for it that day. It means giving your all even when you're not facing an actual competitor and no one is keeping score.

Training properly also means participating in physical activity *consistently*. That means year-round, and not just during the few months when your favorite sport is in season. I play football during a few short months in the fall and winter, but I train every month of the year, even in the off-season, because I know that those extra months of training are going to make me a better-prepared player when the season starts again.

But, here's the thing, I train to play other sports besides football *because training to play other sports makes me a better football player*.

How's that again?

I like to change up my training style during the off-season. For example, in the springs and summers, I practice martial arts. Now, I don't practice *contact* martial arts, but I find that the discipline trains different muscles, or trains the same muscles in different ways. And changing up how I work my muscles, and layering in new and different muscle memories to the way I move, enhances the flexibility of my brain's communication with my body, and ultimately the way I can perform in my primary sport.

There is always some sport in which your kid can participate. Football has a season, but soccer, for example, is a year-round sport, as is the ability to practice martial arts. As I said, I really like having martial arts in my mix of physical activities. And I like it for both the physical workout and the mental discipline it requires. If your kid is struggling with his or her schoolwork, martial arts may be a way to help lift his ability to concentrate and focus his mind, not just his body. But, when you're choosing a teacher for him, make sure to pick an instructor who honors the tradition of his or her art. That is, you don't want the bully who teaches kids to beat the crap out of people, you want someone who understands the finesse, and the grace — you want Mr. Miyagi, not John Kreese. If you check out YouTube you'll find some really cool videos that demonstrate what I'm talking about. For example, the teams that embrace special needs players, like the one coached by Scott Hamilton at Paulding County High School near Atlanta,[1] or the kids that play soccer for JL Mann High in Greenville, South Carolina.[2] Videos like these are testimony to the good that can happen when a coach instills a team mentality, rather than a pack mentality, among his players.

If your primary sport is baseball, try running indoor track — you may just find you've improved on how fast you can run the bases. If your primary sport is wrestling, try gymnastics to improve your strength and balance. If your primary sport is football, you might think about trying basketball to improve lateral quickness and explosion, not to mention hand-eye coordination. It's a fun sport from which your child will gain athletic benefits while continuing to develop skills that will translate to the football field.

Another important reason why your kid should participate in at least one other sport other than his primary one: injury prevention. Pro athletes — and, really, any adult who practices a sport just for the joy and fitness benefits — can injure themselves by straining a muscle or ripping a tendon. Most injuries to adult athletes happen at that spot where the muscle body attaches to the tendon. But young athletes — many of whom are very interested in building

---

1 https://www.youtube.com/watch?v=YnCpnM18g38.

2 https://www.youtube.com/watch?v=A-Rk1dlaxZM.

muscle mass — can rip and tear muscles and tendons right off their growth plates. Varying their activities, and training their muscles in a more "well-rounded" way than is possible when they play only one sport during the year, can help to prevent those kinds of potentially devastating growth-plate injuries.

If you need one more reason to encourage your young athlete to try an off-season activity — well, I'll give you two! First, you need cardio exercise every day of your life. Cardio is especially important for kids in the development of a rich capillary system as they grow. In fact, it's really important for anyone trying to grow muscle at all — if the muscle is richly supplied with capillaries, it's much less likely to cramp. Cardio is also critical to entering adulthood with strong heart health. Fortunately, cardio is an activity you can actually do with your kids — which brings us to my second reason: family fun and bonding. Get a couple of bikes, strap on your helmets, and go for a ride with your daughter. Get a membership to a gym — Planet Fitness and YMCA locations are all over the country and membership is extremely family-affordable — use the treadmills side-by-side and talk to your son while you go a few miles. Put on your sneakers and take a hike with the whole family at a nearby park or wilderness trail. You'll have great experiences together — and set a good example of what lifelong good health habits look like!

Adding a different sport to your kid's schedule adds another level of discipline to his routine, helps to prevent real and possibly distressing injuries to his young body, and adds another level of stamina and endurance to his performance. And it can even be something that makes lifetime parent/child memories.

FREE WEIGHTS VS. MACHINES

Since I mentioned getting a gym membership for your family in the previous section, I think this is a good place to insert a thought or two about weight lifting. First of all, it's important! And I mean that strength training is important for all athletes, not just body builders. Think about it: your muscles are what allow you to make every movement you will ever make in your life. They make it possible for you to throw hard, run fast, jump high — hit a tennis ball farther and more accurately, kick through the water with more speed than your opponent in the next lane, get that extra inch over the other center so you're the one who tips the ball. Of course every athlete needs to hone her muscles with weight training in order to perform to the best of her ability!

More to the point of this book, keeping your muscles well-trained and in tip-top shape is a huge part of injury prevention. Why? Because strengthening your muscles also stresses and strengthens the places where those muscles attach to bone. Keeping that junction between bone and muscle in constant renewal keeps bones strong, dense, and young. So this is another good reason to share a workout with your kid — weight training increases the density of bones, which helps not only to prevent injury, but also to prevent and even reverse osteoporosis in adults.

When your kids start weight training, it's appropriate to have a discussion about what they can expect from the activity — especially in the case of young women athletes. For too long now it has been the conventional wisdom that weight training "bulks you up," and that, I think, has prevented girls and young women from taking up the activity in a way that could really benefit their sports performance. In a nutshell, lifting weights doesn't bulk you up; rather it tones and tightens muscles, making them leaner and stronger. Your muscles will become more dense and toned as a response to training. An increase in size is directly related to nutrition. In order for muscles to grow in size, they need to be fueled with an abundance of protein and carbohydrates. It can, however, increase weight, in that muscle weighs more than fat — that's why it is important that people who take up strength training in order to lose weight understand that a fit body made up of lean muscle may, indeed, tip the scale at a higher number than an unfit body which carries more fat.

I also want to touch on the difference between strength training on machines and doing so with free weights. I use free weights and the reason I do is that, when you use machines, your body is restricted to the path of the machine. That is, your muscles will move only in the way that the machine intends them to move. But when you're doing athletics, you need your body to move in multiple positions and you don't want your muscles to be trained to move in only one path or pattern. Free weights allow you to control the weight and move in a variety of paths.

Now, machines are a great way to get around limitations and still train other muscles and muscle groups when you have been injured, but too often when you go to a gym, the gym's trainer will stick you on the machines and lead you to believe you're getting a full and efficient workout. But, while machines stabilize your body and make working out easier when you're injured, they also make working out easier when you're not injured, and for the same reason — they stabilize your body so you are only using the muscles the machine is designed to work. With free weights your body uses all of its muscles in order to stabilize itself. This works your core, making every exercise more intense and effective.

Sure, it's all right to incorporate some machines into your routine, but they aren't what a good workout is based upon.

There is one caveat to using free weights: you must do so with fierce concentration and careful thought. If you are not paying attention to what you are doing, if you do not engage your entire core purposefully and intentionally as you move a weight through space, and if you haven't been properly trained, you can tear the very tissue you are trying to strengthen. There is a reason my workout pace is so fierce — I am using just as much brain as I am brawn with each session!

SPORTS GEAR

Football players wear shoulder pads, baseball players use mitts, and scuba divers wear wet suits — and they do so for very specific reasons. The areas of the body that need protection vary from sport to sport as the potentials for injuries are different for different kinds of play. That is why athletes and coaches, doctors and designers have, together and over the decades, created specialty gear that not only enhance a player's performance, but offer the most premium amount of protection currently available. As parents, our obligation is to make sure our athletes have not the most expensive or trendiest equipment but the *best fitted, sport-specific* gear.

PROTECTIVE EYEWEAR

Both the American Academy of Pediatrics and the American Academy of Ophthalmology *strongly* recommend that people who participate in sports where there is risk to the eyes wear protective eye gear during play.[1] And what they

---

1 http://www.aao.org/about/policy/upload/Protective-Eyewear-for-Young-Athletes.pdf.

mean is specialized sports eyewear — not street-fashion eyeglasses — that conform to standards set by the American Society for Testing and Materials (ASTM). This is especially important in sports that are high risk for eye injuries like basketball, baseball, softball, and hockey.

MOUTH GUARDS

Right now, the U.S. National Collegiate Athletic Association requires mouth guards to be worn for only four sports — football, lacrosse, ice hockey, and field hockey. But the American Dental Association recommends them for a full twenty-nine sports, including basketball, volleyball, and wrestling.[2] Why? Well, of course to protect a player against broken or chipped teeth, but they actually protect against so much more: lip and tongue injuries, jaw fractures, and even neck injuries and concussions by keeping the lower jaw from smacking into the upper jaw when a player takes a blow to the head. Mouth guards should stay easily in place during play, allow the kid to speak while he's wearing one, and not restrict breathing — in short, they should fit so well that they're *comfortable* in the mouth.

HELMETS

A helmet is standard equipment in my business, as it is for hockey players. While even a well-fitted helmet can't do all that much to protect from the possibility of a concussion, it does protect the scalp and skull, and the brain to some extent, and one that's designed specifically for the sport you play should be SOP — even if there isn't a requirement or a law for it — as should helmets for other sports and

---

2 http://www.ada.org/~/media/ADA/Science%20and%20Research/Files/patient_40.ashx.

activities including bicycling, skateboarding, horseback riding, and skiing.

SAFETY PADS

Shin pads, kneepads, elbow pads, wrist pads, chest pads, neck pads, shoulder pads, hip pads, thigh pads, tailbone shields... If your child plays certain contact sports such as football, lacrosse or hockey, you already know they are mandatory. But well-fitting safety pads, which can prevent cuts and abrasions and reduce the possibility of a sprain or even a fracture after a fall, are just as important for you and your kids when you're participating in other sports and activities where a fall is possible, or even likely, such as inline skating, riding a scooter, or snowboarding.

FOOTWEAR

The right shoes for the right sport can be the difference between spending your post-game time celebrating a win or nursing an injury. Sports that are played on a field — soccer, baseball, football — require cleats for traction and grip. High-tops are the court shoe choice for many basketball players because they offer additional protection for the ankles. Special cycling shoes can increase pedaling efficiency for bicyclers. Whether your kid's sport calls for ice skates or a flexible-soled wrestling bootie, the shoe she wears should be designed specially for her sport to provide the sort of specific support her activity requires, and that shoe should fit her like a glove.

OVERTRAINING?

In 2011 I started Eugene Monroe's Football Camp. It's a program that takes place over the summer, so kids who want to play football can meet, be coached by — and inspired by — pros who were once little kids with big dreams themselves.

At the camp, we expect a lot from the kids — running drills and learning plays, a full day's work and a hard workout, the kind of fun and camaraderie combined with learning and physical tests that most kids relish. And, though it is a full day, we vary the drills so the kids aren't practicing repetitive exercises that could strain their developing bodies. And we make sure the kids are not only well fed but well hydrated, through the course of the camp's day. In these simple, common sense ways, we avoid the problem of *overtraining*— and, of course, it is these common sense solutions you can put in place to make sure your own kids don't "overtrain".

I used quotation marks in the previous sentence because we have to be specific about exactly what we're talking about when we say overtrain. Overtraining is the condition that results when the amount of exercise and the intensity of the exercise exceed a body's ability to recover. When a body can't recover from the workout it has endured, the effect is that the body becomes weaker and loses its capacity to perform at the level it had attained before it got so beaten up.

The first way we can help our kids avoid this condition is to make sure they vary the sorts of exercises they do. Taking part in different sports over the course of the year is a big part of it, but so is making sure they exercise different muscle groups on a day-to-day basis. In bodybuilding, the concept is called "split training" — a method of training in which no more than three muscle groups, or sometimes less, are worked each day, so that the training of different muscle groups is spread out over the course of a multi-day training cycle. In practice, especially for youth athletes, you want to supervise the amount and intensity of the work they do during both practice sessions and games. This means, for baseball players, for example, observing age-appropriate guidelines for limits on how many pitches a player can throw in any game and how much rest he has to have between pitching appearances; we touched earlier in this book on the wisdom of the Little League in imposing strict limits on its players: they do it to protect the players from overtraining and to avoid the shattering growth-plate injuries that could result. For swimmers, this means alternating strokes to avoid the pain and inflammation of swimmer's shoulder, which is the result of the overuse of muscles and tendons. Shin splints and stress fractures are common upshots for soccer players who overuse their lower extremities during the course of practice or play.

Here's the bottom line: when your kid is done working out, or the game is over, he should be pleasantly aware that he's used his muscles. He should feel warm and tired and hungry, and perhaps ready for a hot shower — but he should also feel ready to go home and do his homework, or have fun at family game night, or hang out with his friends and celebrate a win. He *shouldn't* feel so sore and cranky when he comes off the field that he can't participate happily in the next event of his day. If he does, that's a warning sign that he may be overworking his body in an unhealthy way. That's when you, as a parent, need to step in and talk with him and help him figure out why he's hurting. What is lacking in his preparation for play that's making him feel so rotten? The body is not supposed to hurt. It is designed to work and play hard. Persistent pain and soreness are its way of telling you that you aren't treating it right.

THE BIGGER PROBLEM — THE situation in which you really need to worry about your kid's overtraining — is if she's not being fed properly. It is the *under fueling* rather than the overtraining — the lack of adequate nutrition required so her body can both spare the energy she needs to expend on the field and then recover from that expenditure — that is the real cause for concern. If an athlete is underfed, she *can* over train. The best way to understand that statement is to think, again, of your car. When your car needs gas, you fuel up. When it needs an oil change, you change the oil. When the tires are low, you put air in them. Your car will keep running — as long as you give it what it needs. Like a car, the human body can't run on empty.

In the fourth quarter of an NFL game, you can see the players getting tired. We players can see it in each other — we can see the defensive linemen deciding to capitalize on how tired their opponents are. By the end of the season, a lot of the players feel as if they can't give anything more at all. But look at my game — I never get too tired to get the job done. And at the end of the season, I don't collapse — in fact, Nureya has even had to ask me to take a couple of days off! The added stamina isn't because I'm a superhero, it's because I fuel properly. It always all comes back to nutrition, to taking good care of yourself and preparing your body to handle all that you are asking it to do. If you don't eat right while you're training, the positive effects of the work you're doing can turn negative — if you don't keep your tank full, you run the risk of sustaining an injury or just plain burning out.

S–T–R–E–T–C–H !

Tuning into an NFL game, you've surely noticed that when the players take the field at the start of the game, the first thing we do is spread out on our half of the field and stretch out. This practice isn't to give the fans a show. No, we're making sure all of our muscles — our hamstrings, quads, calves, adductor and groin, and back and arm muscles — are as flexible as we need them to be in order to bounce back after the grueling work ahead.

When young kids injure themselves, the injury compounds over time. Think of the tennis champs Serena and Venus Williams who suffer chronic injury and illness as adults because they, famously, over-trained during their youth. Taking enough time to warm up and stretch and get your body balanced before — and after! — a practice session or a day of play goes an enormously long way in helping to prevent overuse and the injuries that can result from it.

Think of the wrist sprains so common among youth and collegiate wrestlers, baseball players, snowboarders and skaters, among others. So many of these sorts of injuries are the result of the athlete twisting or falling on wrist muscles and overstretching ligaments that are rigid because they haven't been properly stretched before play begins. Think of the high ankle sprains that are so common among both youth and pro basketball players. These sprains are extremely painful, often showing color along the outside of the bone and down into the heel, the result of ligaments that have been stretched beyond their limits. The standard remedy for high ankle sprains is lots of ice, and lots of rest — but how much better to avoid such an injury in the first place!

Many young athletes concentrate so much on becoming strong — on lifting ever heavier weights, for example — that they give short shrift to (or forget entirely about) the critical complement to strength: flexibility. There is a Sokhumi proverb that goes, "The wind does not break a tree that bends." A human body that is flexible is less likely to break under stress as well. To bring perfection to strength, our muscles need to be strong *and supple.*

But, in my experience, there is not nearly enough emphasis placed on stretching in either youth sports or in the pros. There usually isn't enough time allotted for this vital exercise in a team setting — maybe twenty minutes at the most; before each game, I spend a minimum of one full hour stretching because I know that a flexible back and hamstrings are the difference between getting hurt and not getting hurt. Flexible muscles don't tear. They don't rip off the bone. They keep me in the game. Even at my size and build, I'm flexible enough to *almost* do a full split, and it is this kind of intense flexibility of muscle that your kid needs to strive for to avoid some of the most preventable injuries in sports. Additionally, providing enough time for pre-game warm-up allows the players to adjust to the temperature in which they're going to be playing — which is critical in preventing both cold- and heat-related illnesses and injuries.

But one of the biggest reasons that stretching before play is so very, very important for young athletes is due to their growth spurts. Their bones may have grown a quarter inch over night — but their muscles and tendons haven't. This means the muscles and tendons will be tight, in comparison to their new height achievement, and they need to focus on stretching the muscles in order to accommodate their new growth so the muscles aren't strained or ripped when they put them to use on the field.

One of the best ways to learn how to stretch properly — and to maintain your body's flexibility — is yoga.

The practice of yoga is simply one of the best methods of improving flexibility — and, as added bonuses, it also strengthens muscles, helps to keep them elastic, and it teaches you how to breathe in ways that help to oxygenate your body.

When you first start yoga practice, no matter how *strong* you are, you are likely to find some of the positions difficult. Don't despair. All good yoga instructors are quick to step right up to help you to modify that position so it's comfortable, and most beneficial, for you. Be mindful that yoga is going to teach you how to use your body differently — it is going to stretch and strengthen your muscles in ways you might not have imagined possible — and that you're in the class to learn and retrain your body. Another critically important technique that is emphasized in yoga is *breathing*. It's vital to remember to breathe during exercise of all types, and yoga puts a spotlight on breathing well and using breath to your advantage while stretching and exercising. Because yoga is such a beneficial practice for the human body, and such a non-competitive way to enhance your physicality, I highly recommend yoga for all ages — you might want to think about signing up for a regular yoga class and taking it *with* your kid, so you can both reap the rewards.

Now, I know that Julie has already discussed hormones in this book, but I want to add some information about the subject as it relates to the all-important objective of flexibility. Specifically, I want to talk about the perceived desirability of the "male" hormone testosterone versus the "female" hormone estrogen, and I guess the first thing I should talk about is that calling one of them male and the other female is a little misleading because each person, no matter his or her gender, has at least a little bit of both. In our culture, however, we tend to think of testosterone as the hormone that makes us tough and forceful and competitive, and a whole long list of other adjectives we typically associate with stereotypical male behavior, and therefore as *the* component most necessary to make a top athlete. Young boys, especially, can get caught up in building muscle mass, and end up increasing their testosterone levels to the point where it's really unhealthy. And why is it unhealthy? Because it is estrogen that helps to keep our bodies flexible — that complements the strength with limberness. A bodybuilder may come off as immense and intimidating, but ask your average muscle man to run a few plays on the football field and he'll soon be begging for mercy. That's because his muscles may look big, but they weren't built to *move*. What athletes really need is a balance of hormones, because a body that is stiff and inflexible is more prone to injury than one that is able to move easily in the full range of human motion.

Finally, I wanted to touch on a real health issue that you've likely seen in the news, and that is teenaged boys who have to deal with low testosterone levels. Please note that there are so many ways to balance a person's hormones without resorting to the use of synthetic hormones that may, themselves, very well have significant influence in triggering unwanted side effects, and even worse conditions and diseases, like cancer. Furthermore, very frequently low testosterone is a symptom, indicating that there is another health problem going on that has to be dealt with; so it is critically important to have any treatment — which is, hopefully, a non-synthetic hormone-replacement approach — supervised by a qualified medical practitioner.

10

SLEEP

 *"*We know sleep is good for us, although scientists are still trying to figure out exactly why... *"*

Sweet slumber! We all do it, we all need it, and most of us enjoy it, though we don't always recognize the benefits of it. Possibly that's because sleep is, in the 21st Century, still a mystery and scientists themselves don't really know exactly why human beings — indeed, all living creatures! — are programmed to be asleep, or at least at rest, for somewhere around a full one-third of our lives.

Among the things we do know, however, is that most adults are sleeping less than we used to a century ago[1] — and that kids are sleeping up to a full hour less per night than they slept just thirty years ago. This lack of adequate sleep, for kids, doesn't only result in the droopy eyes and cranky, sluggish behavior that is such a tip-off in adults who've cut corners on their Z's that it has become a caricature. Lack of adequate rest for a kid can lead to real health as well as social problems.

First, let's talk about the behavioral problems that can result when a child hasn't gotten enough sleep, as they are

---

1 http://harvardmagazine.com/2005/07/deep-into-sleep.html.

different from the behavioral problems sleepy adults manifest. While grown-ups become, as I have already said, cranky and sluggish when they have a sleep deficit, children can often react in the opposite manner, as if they're trying to compensate for being sleepy — becoming hyperactive, easily agitated or jumpy, emotionally and/or physically aggressive; having trouble focusing or concentrating. If these results of sleeplessness sound oddly familiar to you, that's because they're very similar to the symptoms that can often lead to a diagnosis of ADHD. And, indeed, at least one study has revealed that correcting a child's sleep problems can reduce and, in some cases, even actually eliminate the symptoms of ADHD.[1]

NEXT, LET'S TURN our attention to a child's performance in school and how that links with the kid in question getting enough sleep. We grown-ups know that, on the eve of an event such as an important presentation at work or attending our twentieth class reunion, a good night's sleep is going to help make us mentally sharper as well as both be and appear physically rested, so we look our best. A good night's rest can have even more dramatic effects for our kids. Dr. Avi Sadeh of Tel Aviv University found that children who got just one hour more sleep at night performed at higher grade levels than did their peers who went without appropriate sleep. "A loss of one hour of sleep is equivalent to [the loss of] two years of cognitive maturation and development,"[2] Sadeh is quoted as saying about the evidence that well-rested sixth graders perform like sixth graders, but their sleepy counterparts perform only at the fourth-grade level. There is clear evidence that in order for

1 http://www.ncbi.nlm.nih.gov/pubmed/17118097?dopt=AbstractPlus.
2 http://nymag.com/news/features/38951/index1.html.

kids to perform like champs, both in the classroom and on the playing field, they need to be able to sleep like babies.

We'll talk at greater length about hormones later in this chapter; right now, in relation to sleep, I want to talk about certain hormones that help to regulate our children's growth and development. First there's what we commonly refer to as the "human growth hormone," a primary player in our child's over-all development, including how tall she will grow. This hormone is secreted by the pituitary gland and, while it is secreted during the day, the period of the day when it is most intensely released is in stage 3 and stage 4 of sleep.

Then there are the hormones that affect appetite and regulate your child's hunger; inadequate sleep has the potential to change the levels of these hormones in his bloodstream, which can cause overeating and might, with further research, be implicated in the epidemic of childhood obesity and/or lead to type 2 diabetes. Certainly research is telling us that children who don't get enough sleep are prone to weight gain and increased body mass index (BMI).[3]

As I mentioned at the beginning of this section, science is, as I type and however slowly, teasing out the reasons behind the phenomenon of sleep, so it is impossible for anyone to say we know everything we need to know about what happens during our unconscious hours. However, there is this piece of information: it seems our brains detoxify themselves during the course of our sleep.[4]

The body detoxifies itself — that is, gets rid of waste matter — by way of our lymphatic system. Your brain, however, is closed to the lymphatic system — protected, more accurately, from your body's waste — by the blood-brain barrier

3 http://www.bmj.com/content/342/bmj.d2712.
4 http://www.nih.gov/news/health/oct2013/ninds-17.htm.

How Much Sleep?

The Centers for Disease Control and Prevention (CDC) has some good, basic guidelines:[1]

Newborns need 16-18 hours a day.

Preschool-aged children need 11-12 hours a day.

School-aged children need 10 hours a day, minimum.

Teens need 9-10 hours a day.

Adults need 7-8 hours a day.

These are very good guidelines, indeed, but I want to caution you that, as each person is unique, so is his or her need for sleep. Furthermore, sleep can be a dynamic need, meaning that it changes from night-to-night, and can depend on the activities of the day. What do I mean by that? Ever notice how some kids seem to crash on Christmas Day, after the presents are open and the meal is over? Some people lay the blame on the tryptophan in the turkey and, certainly, if you've served turkey for the holiday meal, and your kid is sensitive to the effects, that's part of it.

---

1 http://www.cdc.gov/sleep/about_sleep/how_much_sleep.htm.

that regulates what matter can circulate within your brain and what matter cannot. Studies are now showing that our central nervous system has its own waste disposal mechanism, similar to the lymphatic system, that scientists call the *glymphatic system*. This system works by pumping cerebral spinal fluid through the tissues of your brain, flushing out the waste into your circulatory system so it can be eliminated from your body. But, here's the even bigger news: the glymphatic system really ramps up, functioning at up to ten times its daytime speed, during sleep. And this ramp up coordinates with a shrinkage in brain cells of approximately

Another part of the explanation, however, is that the kids have expended so much energy in tearing open wrapping paper, playing with glittering new toys, enjoying a crowd of cousins and other family members they might not see very often, and *general anticipation* of the day, they crash because they're plumb out of energy. They've used up their stores and need to replenish with some sleep.

If your kiddo has spent a day dealing with stress—the stress of getting excited about a holiday filled with presents and family, or the stress of preparing to take her driver's test, or studying for a big exam, or playing in the big game—she will likely need more than the CDC-recommended amount of shut-eye to recover from it. The good news is that most kids—especially teenaged ones—will naturally sleep, if we let them, as long as they actually need to sleep. Let them. I, too, have waited, often impatiently, for my son to get up and mow the grass on a Saturday morning because, unlike me, he wasn't up at the crack of dawn. But in weighing the benefits to the neighborhood of having the lawn look good three hours earlier than he will get to it, and the benefits to a teenager of a few more hours of sleep, the kid wins out every time.

60%, which allows for more room between brain cells so the cerebral spinal fluid can really get in between them and scrub them clean.

So what kinds of things are scrubbed away? Well, from what we know so far, one of the things that gets scoured out, and in much greater quantities during sleep, is the protein called amyloid-beta that is responsible for forming the plaque found in the brains of Alzheimer's sufferers. The actual cellular structure of our brain changes during sleep, so our body can more efficiently clean it of the waste products that impair its function! Is that some sort of miracle, or what! I, for one, don't need one more reason to get my eight hours a night — or to make sure my kids get their fair share of Zzzzzzs.

SLEEP TIPS

Sleep is important and restorative in so many ways, and our kids — especially our teens — don't do nearly enough of it. If you think about all we are asking of our kids — how taxing it is to grow a fully adult human body, getting through the disruption of puberty, dealing with the emotional stresses of childhood and adolescence, not to mention the stresses of performing well in school and in their respective sports — you can see more clearly how critical it is to get them into bed to get their shut-eye.

So, how do we do that?

First of all: routine, routine, routine! Whether they know it or not (or even consciously *like* it or not), kids crave routine — and authority. It's comforting for them to have someone to whom they look up to setting the rules for them because, intuitively if not always demonstrably, they understand that they don't yet know enough about the world to set the rules for themselves. Set a regular bedtime and enforce it, even on weekends; giving a kid two days worth of "free" bedtime can really screw up their sleep pattern for the entire week. Also, create a predictable bedtime routine for them and be consistent about making sure they perform it — brushing teeth, washing face, saying prayers; this sort of routine not only creates expectations — *after I do this, then I will do this, then I will do this, then I will sleep* — but instills respect for lifelong good health habits.

Incorporate "cool down" activities into the end of the day — things your child can do for thirty minutes or so right before bed, to calm down and relax after an activity-filled day and get him ready for restful sleep. Reading is a classic cool-down/before-bedtime activity — many of us still do it for at least a few minutes before we fall asleep. But do keep the kids away from all screens — TV, mobile phone, computer, and even LED screen e-readers. I use an e-reader much of the time, but the light that emanates from most models isn't restful; a regular, old-fashioned printed book and a nightlight on the table beside the bed is going to be a better bet if you want those eyes to flutter shut.

For some kids, a warm bath or shower works as a cool-down. I recommend this particularly for teenagers. Epsom salts baths are magnificent sources of magnesium and have been long known to help the body detox. In addition, that magnesium will soothe muscles that are sore from a hard workout, practice or game, and magnesium is a great help in getting the mind relaxed and ready to sleep. Bubble baths with lots of toys are a lot of fun for younger kids, with the caveat that bubble baths can be problematic for dry skin, and can contribute to urinary tract infections in girls. But in terms of sleep, there is the possibility that sort of bath can turn into playtime and wind a kid up rather than prepare him for sleep — only you know whether tub time will excite or relax your unique kiddo.

Before you tuck your child in, make sure to draw the curtains in his room, or use blackout blinds — your child's room should feel cozily dark, and be serenely quiet, when it's time to turn out the lights. Some kids demand a night-light and, if that's what you need to do so they're good to sleep alone in their room, well, a parent has to do what a parent has to do; the glow from nightlights, computer screens and the like, however, can filter through eyelids and be a deterrent to restful sleep — and that can mess with a body's internal "clock" and throw off the sleep-wake pattern. Ideally, you can remove these sorts of distractions.

Speaking of clocks, there's a relatively new approach to sleep that has been researched and seems to really help with awakening feeling refreshed. If you set your alarm clock to go off after sleeping in increments of ninety minutes — the length of one sleep cycle — you'll allow your body to complete its natural rhythm of sleep cycles rather than being abruptly awakened in the middle of a sleep cycle.[1] A good night's sleep consists of five to six complete sleep cycles. Our household found that we all awaken so much more pleasantly and easily using one of the many apps that tell you what time to go to bed based on what time you have to wake up. All of the apps allow fifteen minutes to fall asleep, and I have been amazed at how easy it is to get out of bed when I have completed a sleep cycle. You'll find a link to a web site that allows you to calculate the time you'll need to set your alarm based on your bedtime, and optimum sleep cycles, in the Resources section of this book. And, of course, multiple apps are available to download to your phone.

I'm also an advocate of removing temptation from the kids' rooms at night. Electronics that continually emit signal are increasingly being recognized as a source of potentially profound negative impact on our health — so much so that we'll talk about it in detail in the next section. But this is especially true for our children who, because they are smaller people, have much higher uptake of radiation from electronics. Furthermore, to expand on what I was saying about e-Readers, the LED screens are so bright that they confuse the brain about whether its day or night and can really disrupt sleep. For this reason, phones, iPads, and iPods stay in the family room overnight so there's no

---

1 http://www.nature.com/nature/journal/v497/n7450_supp/full/497S2a.html

urge to text back a friend who has a later bedtime schedule, or to play one or two more games of Temple Run after Mom and Dad leave the room.

All that said, the solution to good sleep for kids isn't, unfortunately, always easy. Researchers at the Texas Children's Hospital's Sleep Center estimate that up to a full 37% of children[2] from kindergarten age through fourth grade have sleep problems or disorders ranging from trouble falling asleep or staying asleep and sleepwalking, to sleep seizures and other neurological disorders that can impact their ability to sleep, and/or the quality and quantity of sleep the child is capable of on a routine basis. If none of the tips and tricks outlined above work for you, you will want to talk to your child's doctor about your child's sleep issues, or even visit a sleep center that specializes in childhood sleep problems. From melatonin to start sleep, to good quality 5HTP to continue sleep, to glycine, theanine, valerian root and chamomile teas, and that magnificent mineral, magnesium, there are a whole host of natural approaches that can help our children get good, restorative rest.

---

2 http://www.texaschildrens.org/Locate/Departments-and-Services/Neurology/Neurophysiology/Sleep-Center/.

11

ELECTROMAGNETIC RADIATION

 *"*And one more thing: EMR…*"*

There's just one more thing we need to talk about at this point relative to prevention, and that's EMR, or *electromagnetic radiation*.

We've already discussed that it is exposure to outside forces of other chemicals that does damage to our biochemistry. Those other chemicals include the ones that big agricultural companies use to grow most of the food that is sold in grocery store produce sections and that then make their way into our bodies when we consume the fresh but petro-chemically fertilized strawberries we slice up to put on our children's cereal in the morning, or the petro-chemically fertilized potato that was used to produce our processed potato chips. Chemicals that make up the sort of standard cleaning products most of us use to mop our kitchen floors or scrub our toilet bowls, uncapped and released into the air for us and our families to breathe in, diluted in water into which we plunge our naked hands and making their way into our bodies by way of the pores in our skin. Chemicals in our soaps and shampoos, in the cotton in our child's shirt, the desk at which she sits to do her homework and other furniture in our homes, the air around us in the form of car exhaust pipes and industrial smokestacks and second-hand smoke. Even the *biochemicals* that our own bodies produce can turn against us when we are overworked and overwhelmed — that is, under stress.

But there is another source of those pesky free radicals, and that is electromagnetic radiation. Though we are only just beginning to recognize their role in causing health problems, UV rays, microwaves, and other sorts of electromagnetic radiation our kids come in contact with on a daily basis can be the cause of cancers and other illnesses.

Sunlight, the cause of painful sunburn, is one source of EMR with which we are all familiar — and the reason we are all so diligent about slathering our kids with sunscreen before they head outdoors. But there are so many other sources that bombard us with radiation these days — the wireless mouse and keyboard of our computer, the router in our home generating our Wifi, our cell phones continuously as they search for nearby towers unless we turn them off or put them on airplane mode, our myriad handheld devices, the microwave oven, the fancy console in our new car that does everything for us but wipe our kid's nose and kiss him goodbye as we drop him off at school. These are all sources of electromagnetic energy that gets inside our bodies, assaults our cells, and generates free radicals.

How?

There are three acronyms with which we need to be familiar to discuss the next part of the answer: EMR, EMF, and SAR. EMR, as we've already covered, stands for ElectroMagnetic Radiation that is both emitted by and absorbed by charged particles. The phrase, 'charged particles' should sound familiar to you — these are the atoms that either donate or, like free radicals, are looking for electrons.

EMF stands for ElectroMagnetic Field, or an atmosphere created by those charged particles. EMR, the radiation, occupies or exists as an EMF, the field. The terms, while different to a physicist, are fairly interchangeable to the lay person. Radiation can be ionizing, such as the radiation that is used to kill cancer cells, meaning that it has enough energy to remove tightly bound electrons from atoms, thus creating ions. It can also be non-ionizing, meaning that it has only enough energy to move atoms around and make them vibrate. Microwave ovens are one type of non-ionizing EMR, but many if not most of our electronic tools and toys emit microwave EMR to function.

At this point, the next question you will be asking yourself is, *How does EMF relate to me?* Well, the human body absorbs EMR and, as you might expect, just thinking intuitively, absorbing radiation that moves around the atoms inside our bodies might not be a very good thing for the human body to be asked to do very often. Since our most significant source of EMR exposure is probably our cell phones, I'm going to focus on them as my primary example for the purposes of learning about EMR.

SAR— our final acronym— stands for Specific Absorption Rate. It is very specifically a measure, in watts per kilogram (W/kg), of the EMR absorbed by living tissue when it is exposed to EMF/EMR. In most studies that measure SAR, researchers are looking at brain tissue that has been exposed to the EMR coming off a cell phone in use.

Europe, Australia, and the US, among other countries, have set limits for the amount of SAR that can be emitted from cell phones; interestingly, the European standards are less stringent than the US and Australia but, critically, those standards were created based upon the subject, or recipient, of SAR as a relatively large and weighty adult male, and the object generating the EMR as a 900 mHz phone. The limit set in the US is that no more than 1.6W/kg averaged over 1 gram of tissue should be absorbed by the adult male head and trunk when using a cell phone.[1] But understanding what this standard means is complicated, because when you use a cell phone, there is variation in how much EMR is emitted depending on *how* and *where* and *who* is using the phone. Texting, for example, emits a lower amount than speaking. The distance you are from a cell tower when the phone is in use is yet another variable that will impact SAR values. What is even more essential to the calculation of SAR in any particular instance, however, is to understand that the absorption rate will be different for humans with less mass and weight than the standard industry subject. There is a much higher SAR in children, *as much as 153% more*, than in adults.[2]

There has been much discussion about SAR and whether or not it is damaging to humans, and there are discrepancies in the research that has been done. There have been studies that find there are no significant problems and others that find there are issues with SAR, and these have all been dutifully — and confusingly — reported in the media. What is compelling is that a group of researchers from all over the world came together in 2009 to co-author a paper that discussed the significant concerns about EMR and its potential to cause cancer, especially brain tumors. The authors very specifically discussed the industry's own findings, their bias, and the flaws in their research.[3] They voiced very specific concerns that SAR significantly

---

1 http://www.fcc.gov/encyclopedia/specific-absorption-rate-sar-cellular-telephones.

2 http://informahealthcare.com/doi/abs/10.3109/15368378.2011.622827; http://www.iaeng.org/publication/WCE2010/WCE2010_pp759-763.pdf; http://www.ncbi.nlm.nih.gov/pubmed/22005525.

3 http://www.radiationresearch.org/pdgs/reasons_us.pdf.

contributes to causing cancer, especially brain cancer, and offered theories as to how and why it might happen.

Now, because the initial SAR research has been conducted on brain tumors, does that mean that SAR impacts only the brain? Unfortunately, no. There are, for example, increasing reports of multi-focal breast cancer in very young women. One story I found compelling was presented at a conference I was attending: a twenty-something-year-old tri-athlete exercised with her cell phone carefully tucked into the special cell phone pocket in her sports bra. She developed four different tissue types of breast cancer right below the area where the phone was carried in the center of her chest — a very unusual location for breast tumors.

So where does this information leave us? There are not a lot of double-blinded, placebo-controlled trials looking at cancers and other diseases that might have been caused by exposure to EMR— *yet*. And some medical people think that this means there is no evidence-based medicine to support the possibility that cell phone EMR might be contributing to illness. But we need to remember that, similarly, there are no double-blinded, placebo-controlled trials supporting the use of a parachute to counter the effect of gravity when jumping out of airplanes. In fact, using parachutes has, in terms of the quality of its evidence, been given an "F" grade by the medical field. This fact was actually published in the medical literature[4]— look at the footnote; I am not making that up. And, yet, given the choice, we would all likely prefer to have access to a parachute if we were jumping out of an airplane, despite the lack of double blind placebo controlled trials, aka "good medical evidence," that a parachute might be useful on our way down.

---

4   http://www.ncbi.nlm.nih.gov/pubmed/16602356.

So what does that mean for us parents? Banning electronic devices outright — and prying our kids' cell phones and tablets and laptops out of their cold, freaked-out hands? If your kids are anything like mine, that scenario probably wouldn't end well.

Talk to your kids about the safe use of electronic devices. Impress upon them the importance of using wired headphones or putting the caller on speaker *every* time they talk on the phone — that is, don't allow the phone to make direct contact with their heads. Make sure they don't carry their phones in the pockets of their clothing — cell phones tucked into the pockets of jeans, for example, mean that the wearer is, in essence, microwaving him- or herself all day long, frying penises, testicles or ovaries. Put a limit on how many hours they can use a computer or a tablet during the course of the day, so they don't spend every waking hour in an environment that's drenched with EMR.

Which brings me to another aspect of EMR — other consequences to the extensive use of cell phones and all of these electronic tools that have less to do with direct cellular damage and more to do with contribution to the stress of living in the electronic age. There are behaviors we have developed as a result of cell phone and computer use that weren't present in days gone by. When I was a child, my house had a rotary phone that had neither call waiting nor an answering machine attached to it. When it rang, we answered it and, if the requested party wasn't in, we took a message — and got in trouble with Mom or Dad if we didn't do it right. Certainly we didn't begin rapidly redialing or frantically texting someone if we didn't get an immediate and instantly gratifying response. But in our electronic age, you don't touch someone else's phone, never mind answer it. It's a given: the phone is always for you — after all, it's *your* phone. We come unglued when the flight atten-dant tells us we have to turn off our phones on the airplane, and we check our messages and texts as soon as the wheels of the airplane touch the ground again. These individual-use devices that are on our bodies all day long are running our lives. They add a sense of stress and urgency and per-suade us with their endless notifications and ringtones that they come first, before any human interaction. They inter-rupt conversations, they supplant normal communication between people, and they are absolutely genuinely addic-tive.[1] When a phone rings or vibrates or beeps, we all stop what we are doing or thinking or saying to be sure that what's happening electronically isn't more important than what we are currently doing in the here and now.

It's gotten a little out of hand, hasn't it?

Actually, "out of hand" is part of the solution. We need to get our electronics off our bodies, out of our hands, away from our heads, and out of our consciousness — so they aren't ranking first, in front of everything else in our lives. We need to be able to unplug, disconnect, and get back to breathing, sleeping, and living a less frantic, urgent, over-driven lifestyle.

Set some policies for your kids — and for yourself, too, if you need them — to wean yourselves, for at least a few hours every day, from your devices. As a physician who is on call 24/7, I recognize what a challenge this can be, but I've made it a priority for my family to manage this at least a few hours every week. Some good ground rules to try? The kids' cell phones are on airplane mode when they're doing homework — no interruptions! — and they are allowed to be in the vicinity of a tablet or a computer while they're working on schoolwork only if they're using the

---

1 http://www.biomedcentral.com/1471-2458/11/66

device to do school-related research or type a paper. Phones are on airplane mode, as well, every night during dinner, so the kids can participate in the conversation around the table and not the ones their friends are having via text messaging. Phones are also on airplane mode during family game night, when we're watching a movie together in the family room, and on family car trips so we're all in the adventure together — having the same conversation or listening to the same music — rather than isolated in our separate seats, behind separate sets of earbuds. I admit, this has meant that I have listened to some music I definitely didn't entirely enjoy — I am an old school rock and roll girl in the car and hip hop just doesn't do it for me; but listening to my kids' music, with them, while we travel in the car, has made for some great discussions, a lot of funny banter, and more than one priceless insight into those things that my kids find important or are trying to deal with. These policies — not accepted initially with ease — have helped us all be more completely *with* each other, more present in each other's lives, and are totally worth the early struggle.

12

RECOGNIZING WHEN AN INJURY HAS HAPPENED

"We are our kids' first line of defense."

Julie has talked at length in the previous pages about how important it is to find a pediatrician who believes in the value of well visits. Who will, at a well visit, spend all the time he or she needs to spend to not only examine your child physically, but talk to both you and your child so his understanding of all the factors that make up your child's ability to stay healthy as he grows and develops is as complete as it is possible to be. Someone who will not just gather data about your child annually, but who knows how to interpret all of that data and provide answers and advice about it. And who has the sports medicine background to care competently for an active, sports-oriented child — making sure that your athlete isn't anemic, but has everything she needs to truly thrive. When it comes to your kid's health, his doctor is — to use a metaphor Julie and I cited in the opening of this book — the ace up your sleeve. He or she is the expert whose training you rely on to guide you as your child grows, and whose phone number you probably have on speed dial — *just* in case of emergency.

Of course, your doctor isn't the only person in your child's life upon whom you rely to help you protect and monitor your child's well being. Teachers, coaches, grandparents, even the parents of your kid's friends — these are all people to whom you entrust your child's care. As with so much in life — as with functional medicine itself — so much needs to be in harmony for the system you've set in place to perform efficiently, and there are overlaps all over the place. But, at the end of the day, we parents are our kids' first line of defense. Most of us see and spend time with our children every day, so we're in the best position to observe any changes in the way they conduct themselves physically, mentally, emotionally or developmentally that might be cause for concern. And, because we parents are our children's fiercest advocates, we're in the best position to react appropriately when we notice those changes.

So, given that most of us aren't physicians ourselves, or experts in sports medicine, what's the best advice for appropriately evaluating how our kids are doing? How much we are asking of them — especially when it comes to their participation in sports — and how they're handling it? The best advice is to remember that they are kids — and to remember that we're not evaluating a person who is our physical peer, someone who can handle the same sorts of stresses that we can, or absorb the same sorts of blows. We're evaluating *kids*.

Let's talk about all the ways in which our kids are vulnerable.

First, their bodies aren't yet very big or strong. Their bones are still hardening and lengthening, their growth plates are open, and their organs, while benefitting from reserves we grown-ups should envy, aren't very heavy.

Then we layer in athleticism and we've got to be even more thoughtful about how we help them care for their bodies — feeding them the fuel they need, making sure they get adequate sleep, buying them the protective gear their sport calls for, developing a rapport with their coach and assessing her ability — her wisdom — to guide our child and safeguard him while he's under her supervision.

If our child is underweight — and lots of kids can be at one or another stage of their unique development — then we have to take that into consideration as well. You'll notice that it is often the "skinny" folks who get injured, straining or tearing muscles, and that's because they have little body fat to protect them.

When an injury does occur, there's the danger of scarring, so that's a fourth level of vulnerability. Scar tissue is not elastic, tears easily, and requires a lot of maintenance. When I had breast cancer, and all of the surgery that went with it, more than five years ago, the scar tissue in my chest and my armpits became my main post-operative focus. Massage was my solution, weekly, and to this day, if I don't have massage regularly, I really still feel the scars pulling.

And those are just a start. Eugene has already explained that it is impossible to wrap up the brain in such a way that it can be completely protected from any blow or during any fall — helmets can protect the skull, but the brain is still swimming around inside of it like a rubber duck in a cooler. And, even if we could wrap up our gray matter in bubble wrap, that still wouldn't do a darned thing to mitigate the enormous changes that naturally happen to it during childhood and adolescence.

When a baby is born, his brain contains about *one hundred billion neurons*, or brain cells. All of these billions of cells are primed and ready to go, but few of them are *connected*. The brain, at this age, is sort of like a construction zone at the beginning of the build — all the raw materials have arrived and are neatly laid out, the bricks and the mortar and such, but each in a separate pile waiting to be put together to create the house or the office building or church they're meant to be.

For about the next three years, her brain will focus on building around *one thousand trillion synapses* out of these raw materials, and the stimulus for the construction will be sensory stimuli: the sound of a bird singing, or her mother talking to her; the smell of food cooking in the kitchen, or her father's aftershave; the sight of a red balloon; the feel of the family dog licking her face. These stimuli cause the brain cells to start talking to one another and form connections. When the stimuli is repeated frequently enough — hearing the sound of her mother's voice every day, for example — those neural connections become very strong.

Things really start to happen when, from age three to age eleven, the brain, now dense with neural networks, voraciously sucks in new learning experiences. Fine motor skills develop, language blossoms, sensory functions are refined, emotional control begins, the brain growing ever richer and more complex.

Then, at around age eleven, the brain really begins to aggressively prune itself — the neural networks that are seldom used vanish, and the ones that are used more often become stronger, denser, more efficient, permanent parts of the growing adult brain structure. As the healthy brain matures, neural impulses flow ever more smoothly throughout the brain, allowing for information to be integrated across the various brain regions that work together to control cognitive, motor, and emotional functions. All of this happens because of the physical structure, or architecture, of the brain — such factors as the integrity of the junctures between brain synapses, the diameter of the axons, the thickness of the myelin.

One of the reasons I not only allow but encourage my own children to participate in sports is that I believe athletics help give our kids a mental edge. Like the rest of the body, the brain needs the benefits of physical exercise to work its best. The benefits of, specifically, *aerobic* exercise are myriad.[1] We generally talk about this sort of exercise in terms of "getting the blood flowing." But what actually happens when we raise our heart level and get the blood pumping faster through our veins? Well, the flow of oxygen and nutrients to the brain improves, and the level of neurotransmitters increases — which, among other things, influences our memory. And the implications of an improved memory are that doing a little cardio can mean our kids get better grades in school — and that we older folks don't lose our car keys or forget what we went to the grocery store to buy.

But the benefits to the brain of doing sports aren't only physical. Athletics also help to workout our kids' *mental muscles*, if you will, because learning new rules and new skill sets help to form new neural networks in their developing brains. Playing sports is another experience that enriches the density and complexity of the brain structure itself and

---

1 Aerobic (meaning with oxygen) exercise, commonly known as cardio, means exercise that uses oxygen to meet the energy demands of the workout — speed walking, jogging, biking, for example. Aerobic activity can be done continuously without a break. Anaerobic (meaning without oxygen) exercise is what happens when the body is pushed so hard that the energy generation exceeds what can be made aerobically and energy also gets made without oxygen — it often happens at that point in the workout that is concentrated on building muscle mass, weight lifting, for example. Anaerobic exercise requires breaks in activity and is thought to be part of the reason for muscle soreness after intense exercise.

can, therefore, profoundly impact who our children can become.

Keep in mind, however, as we discussed in Part One and in the best estimation of current science, the brain won't "finish" developing — won't come into its full, dense and complex cognitive capacity — until sometime in the child's mid-twenties. Truthfully, the brain is probably never completely finished developing, but the bulk of the work seems to take a full two decades. And this fact brings us to the fifth and final level of vulnerability a child faces: that the lack of full cognitive ability means the lack of the ability to make the best judgments and competently assess risk. Indeed, because of what we now know about how the brain grows and develops over the course of nearly the whole first quarter century of a person's life, some experts are calling for a reassessment of the juvenile justice policy. "[B]ecause of their immature brains, adolescents may be more likely to engage in reckless and sensation-seeking behavior — and to get involved in criminal activity,"[1] explained Columbia Law School professor and author of the book *Rethinking Juvenile Justice*, Elizabeth S. Scott.

So how does all of this translate into your protecting your vulnerable young athletes? What can you do to help them prevent injury — and, importantly, how does it help you to recognize when they are injured?

In my role as physician to my NFL players, one of my primary responsibilities is to watch them play — in games and, as often as I can, in practice. I watch for how they're walking and how they're running, where they get hit — and how hard, how fatigued they appear by the fourth quarter. I'm watching to see if they're limping, favoring an arm, standing normally, shifting weight differently, running out

---

1 http://www.law.columbia.edu/media_inquiries/news_events/2013/july2013/scott-brain-research.

of steam too early in the game. I do this so I know how to treat them at the end of it. Fortunately for me, this responsibility is also a pleasure.

Just as fortunately for us parents, most of us take a great deal of pleasure in watching our kids play their chosen sport or sports. We sit in the stands and cheer for each touchdown, each basket, each base hit. And if the ball crosses home base without getting slammed by the bat — that is, if it connects with our kid's knee instead of ending up in the catcher's mitt — we are the first ones on the diamond, checking out the extent of the injury.

Our first line of defense in helping to prevent injury is to simply do what most of us are already doing! It is to watch our kids play, of course, but to do it even more mindfully than we do now. I do *not* mean you should rush out to the field every time you see your son shaking out his hands after a pitch, or rubbing his shin when he gets out from under a pile on the football field. But I do mean that you make a mental note that it happened, and then notice if he does it again — maybe a little later in the same game, or maybe next week at a different game altogether. Look for clues that he's favoring his right leg, or she doesn't seem to have the same range of motion in her swimming stroke, or her sister isn't gripping the bat quite as confidently as she had just the game before. Small changes like these could mean something as mundane as your kid is having a bad day at play, but hints like these could also be indications that something is strained or sprained or otherwise not working as well as it should. And by noting the small things, when the problems they could indicate are also likely still small, you can take the proactive steps that will keep them from becoming big things.

> "Getting an athlete to talk about an injury? That's the hard part."

When you play professional sports, you get used to getting hurt, and you start to think being hurt is normal. You still have to practice, you still have to play — just like almost everyone else the whole world over, no matter how bad you might feel, you still have to get up out of bed, take a shower, and go to work.

In my particular line of work I know that even when my teammate tells me he's feeling fine, his knees are throbbing with every step. I, myself, have insisted that I'm feeling OK after a game even when I know that something's not right. As athletes we're programmed not to think about our injuries because, even if we're injured, we still have to perform. Since I met Julie, however, I don't get away with saying *I'm good* when I'm really not. For example, a few years ago she noticed that after the games I was rubbing my neck and my left knee more than she thought I ought to be if I really was as good as I was claiming, and she insisted I get myself checked out. We discovered that I actually had sustained an injury. So she set me up with a program of exercise and other therapies, and we really got aggressive about healing the problem during the off season. The work paid off.

Let's face it: I'm more valuable to my team when I'm on the field *and* focusing on fighting the opposing team rather than the pain in my neck or elsewhere in my body. And I know that, because of early intervention, I can be confident that I've already begun to address any issues I've accumulated through a lengthy sports career and enter eventual retirement in good health.

I've also had a few concussions that I didn't want to face up to. All of them were bad — and what I mean by that is that *all* concussions are bad, even if some of them aren't classified as concussions. Let me be very clear about this: you can have a concussion and not lose consciousness! But the worst one for me — well, you know, you're running a play, you're on automatic, "head hunting," cleaning up for the ball carrier, and in the end a three-hundred-and-thirty-pound defensive lineman wants you on the ground? I got blindsided — my head got hit and then, even worse, my head hit the ground.

I got up and continued to play. But, after the game, both Nureya and Julie knew something was very wrong because I wasn't acting like myself. I, however, didn't want to take what had happened to me too seriously. First of all, when you play football as a kid, you get used to getting hit in the head and having your teammates, and even your coaches, brush it off or make a joke out of it: "Oh, he just got his bell rung!" Second, as a pro player, you understand that taking a hit is just part of doing business and you don't whine about it any more than, say, an insurance salesman whines about having to do the paperwork of filing claims. You may not like it, but it's all just part of the job.

But Nureya and Julie took it seriously even if, because of the concussion itself, I was in no state of mind to deal with the fact that a head injury is just never a joking matter. Julie reminded me that what had just happened to my brain had the potential to cause life-changing problems; however, if I stopped trying to deny I was hurt, and we treated it quickly and correctly, there was no need for the injury to be long-term. So, of course, we treated it.

Pro-football players can expect to take a hit every time they take the field. It isn't unrealistic to think that some of them get a concussion every day they play. It isn't so very different for youthful players of sports.

Nor are kids generally very different from their grown-up counterparts in their reluctance to report an injury. One of the benefits of our young people participating in organized sports is that it teaches them to be "tough," a good quality that will serve them well as they walk through life — depending on how you define "tough." If what we mean is that participating in sports teaches kids to stretch beyond their current capabilities to reach a goal, then we're getting what we want. But if we mean that we press them so hard to be strong and resolute and competitive that they become numb to pain — we're not doing our kids any favors.

It's up to us parents to make our kids feel comfortable talking about their health. To ask them how they're feeling *after* a game — and, if we have noticed our child standing, moving, or behaving in a way that doesn't fit the way the child normally acts or behaves, not to accept "fine" as an answer.

During the game is a whole different story. An injury — especially a head injury — won't always take a child out of the game, even when it should. These are the times when a parent has to step in and be the bad guy, if necessary. Unless an injury is dramatic, a player, almost by definition, won't take herself out of the game. Someone who knows the child well, and knows how she typically moves and behaves, can see a problem — often more clearly than even the coach.

So, if you suspect your kid has sustained a head injury, how do you know when to take him out of the game?

- He says he feels "slow," when you ask him how he feels, or he uses words like "heavy" or "fuzzy" to describe the sensation of not knowing quite how to open a car door or use the phone, or he needs an extra second to recognize a familiar face or thing.
- He has become sensitive to light or to noise.
- He is feeling dizzy or is having trouble balancing and seems to be moving in slow motion.
- He experiences blurred vision, or is having trouble hearing you when you speak.
- He has a headache.
- He experiences nausea or vomiting.
- He becomes more emotional and demonstrates unusual irritability, sadness, or anxiety.
- His sleep patterns are disrupted — he is sleeping more than he normally does, or less than he normally does, or he is unable to fall asleep at all.

I depended on Nureya and Julie to see that I was acting differently than I normally do when I had my concussion because, after you get hit in the head, you are really not in the right state of mind to decide if you're "fine" or not. A kid (or adult) who gets hit in the head is really not going to be able to make a wise decision about whether or not he should keep on playing. This is when he is going to depend on you, his parent, to make the call.

STEROIDS AND OTHER PERFORMANCE-ENHANCING SUBSTANCES

The use of steroids to increase athletic performance is, flatly, cheating. It is taking a dangerous shortcut instead of doing the hard work that athletic excellence truly requires.

And, unfortunately, it is also nothing new. No matter that the subject is still a popular one in the media today — the discovery of another pro athlete using steroids; another report on CNN about the dangers of steroid use for young people — steroids were first developed in the 1930s. They were first used to boost a sports performance by Soviet weightlifters at the 1952 Helsinki Olympics where they easily broke all of the world's weightlifting records.

Most of us parents don't know a lot about steroids and how they're used to enhance athletic performance — most of us don't need to. Depending on your source, use of steroids for this purpose by young people — kids between fourteen and eighteen years old — is somewhere between 2.7% and 4%. Pretty low, right? Except that when you turn the percentages into actual numbers, that comes out to about six hundred and fifty thousand kids who use steroids for non-medical purposes in any given year. And not only boys are involved — a little less than 1% of teenage steroid users are girls. But whether it's boys or girls — that's about six hundred and fifty thousand kids too many.

The place to start talking about steroids is to make the distinction between the two classes of them — and these classes are *corticosteroids* and *anabolic steroids*. Corticosteroids, such as the more well known asthma drug prednisone, are derived from adrenal-sourced hormones, and they're used in medicine primarily to suppress inflammation and to treat certain pain conditions. Anabolic, or androgenic steroids also have a place in medicine — they are sometimes used to reverse anemia or to treat patients who have had severe chronic illness or certain conditions such as delayed puberty or breast cancer. But they also have a more nefarious — and *illegal*— purpose: to artificially accelerate growth in order that the user ends up with less body fat, bigger muscles, and more strength.

Anabolic-androgenic steroids — known also as AAS or, at the street level, "roids" and "juice", and by such common brand names as Androsterone, Decadurabolin, Oxandrin, and Equipoise — are manmade substances that are related to the male sex hormone testosterone. They are commonly taken either orally or by way of injection into muscle, and they work in the body by making their way to the hormone receptors in the cell. There they trigger a message to the cell's DNA to make specific proteins that stimulate the anabolic, or growth, response.

It is a no-brainer that playing around with your DNA on a cellular level isn't a very smart thing to do, and the effects of these drugs on the human body go way beyond deceptively pumped up muscles. For boys — because the body stops making natural testosterone when it detects the artificial stuff — the use of anabolic steroids shrinks the testicles, lowers sperm count, causes male-pattern baldness, and increases breast size. For girls, the side effects of excess fake testosterone increases the growth of body hair, roughens the skin, deepens the voice, and decreases breast size. Both genders are equally affected by other dangers:

+ high blood pressure and the risk of stroke
+ increased levels of LDL, or bad cholesterol
+ decreased levels of HDL, or good cholesterol
+ skin infections that can become more dangerous if the batch of the illegal drug is infected by bacteria
+ HIV, if users are sharing needles
+ liver disease, including liver cancer
+ acne

- behavioral problems such as rage, violence, mania, aggression, and delusion
- addiction

Just in case you think these sorts of performance-enhancing substances are a problem only among kids who've got money to spare, a product called creatine is available to bodybuilder wannabes on a budget. While not an anabolic steroid, the side effects of creatine can include muscle compartment syndrome, a fairly serious condition in which increased pressure builds up in certain muscle groups; eventual muscle breakdown — which can increase risk of muscle injury; abnormal heart rhythms; and sudden kidney failure.

Building muscle isn't something that happens overnight. It takes a healthy diet as well as work at the gym to create authentic strength and definition. I can't speak to the motivations that lead a grown person to get into these sorts of dangerous and illegal drugs, but, as Julie has already pointed out, kids aren't known for their capability in making sound life judgments — and sometimes a kid wants to bulk up so badly that he'll take the risk. This is where, again, a parent needs to intervene. How can you tell if your kid is at risk?

- His complexion is oily, or he is getting more than his usual share of adolescent pimples.
- He has bulked up noticeably in a short amount of time.
- He is acting aggressively or has bouts of rage.
- You find needles in his room or needles are found in his school or gym locker room.

If you notice any of these symptoms, talk with your kid. But please don't insist he simply stop taking the substance, cold turkey. Depending on the length of time he's been using the drug, the withdrawal period could be difficult for him and include thoughts of suicide. Even worse, abrupt withdrawal, like what might happen if an athlete were hospitalized or went on a family vacation, can so destabilize body chemistry that there is a risk of death if the medical team doesn't know what the body is missing. Consult with your family doctor about support for your child while he goes through the ordeal of withdrawal.

That's a lot of bad news. As I've said, not many parents will have to deal with steroid use, and for the ones who will, the good news is that once a child is weaned from the drug, he will look, and act, like himself once again.

13

HEALING

 " If you don't break it, you don't have to fix it. *"*

Aha! *Healing!* Finally! Some readers are going to think of this — the part where we talk about how to fix something that's broken — as the most important section of the book. Allow me to disagree. There are hundreds of different ways to injure the human body while playing sports, and there is one way to avoid putting in the cost, time, inconvenience, and pain of rehabilitation: prevent the problem in the first place. That's why we've spent so many pages talking about things like the importance of a healthy diet, supplying proper sports equipment, and s-t-r-e-t-c-h-i-n-g.

But the nature of sport — the nature of exuberant, high-energy play — means that high ankle sprains, swimmer's shoulder, tennis elbow, and even concussions are going to be facts of life for some athletes, even when we take the most proactive prevention measures. So let's talk about the most common complaints and injuries that our young athletes have to deal with, and how we can best help them to recover.

MUSCLE SORENESS

Aching muscles can be caused by several medical conditions, including rheumatoid arthritis, fibromyalgia, chronic fatigue syndrome, and even a bout of the flu or a cold. Mild muscle soreness and stiffness after a workout, on the other hand, are commonplace and not worrisome because they are merely an indication that the muscles have been used.

The best way to treat sore muscles is the time-honored, twenty-minute soak in a warm bath to which two generous cups of Epsom salt has been added. Our grandmothers might not have known *why* an Epsom salt bath works, but they were right that it does. That's because the primary "ingredient" of Epsom salt is magnesium, a mineral that, unlike other minerals, can be absorbed transdermally, or through the skin. Among the various other functions it performs in the body, magnesium significantly mitigates the factors that lead to muscle ache by flushing out the lactic acid that can build up in muscles during an intense workout. Magnesium also helps the body to more efficiently absorb nutrients, so a healthy, after-game snack of a vitamin-laden protein shake and a soak in an Epsom salt bath should give your sore player great relief.

MUSCLE CRAMPS

If your player has stretched out well before a game, and remains hydrated during play, she shouldn't have a huge problem with muscle cramps. However, let's talk about how she stays hydrated. She needs the right kind of liquid in her body, and most athletes swig "sports drinks" all through a game to relieve their thirst, which are, by and large, exactly the *wrong* things to drink. Read the ingredients on the labels of those "sports drinks" and what you'll

How to Make an Ice Pack

There are all sorts of commercial ice packs on the market, but you don't need fancy to be effective. You can make your own ice packs at home, and I actually prefer the homemade sort because they're inexpensive and, because of the amount of solution in the bag, they can be more easily molded around the injury. Here's how to do it.

You'll need one cup of rubbing alcohol, two cups of water, a gallon-sized plastic freezer bag, and a kitchen towel.

Pour the rubbing alcohol and the water into the bag and close the bag tightly, taking care to squeeze the air from the bag as you close it. Place the bag in the freezer for at least one hour before you use it. Wrap the cold bag in the kitchen towel before placing it on the injury. When you're done using it, return it to the freezer so it's ready for the next time.

Another trick, for when you need an ice pack in a hurry—simply keep a bag of frozen peas or nibblet corn on hand, wrap the whole bag in a kitchen towel and use that as your makeshift but super-effective ice pack.

find prominently listed are sodium and some form of sugar. What makes sense about putting salt and sugar into an athlete when what he needs are magnesium and calcium? A protein shake to fuel his body during the game, and water to quench his thirst, are much better choices. And don't even get me started on kids who chug down an "energy drink" on the sidelines — the kids may enjoy the "high" those sorts of beverages cause, but they are incredibly *dehy*drating and cause, as well, other harmful side effects such as sleeplessness, nausea, irritability, increased heart rate and blood pressure, and abnormal heart rhythms.

Taking a longer view, the off-season is a great time to prevent for cramps. Many times, cramps occur when muscles have been quickly developed with aggressive weight lifting, but without adequate cardio. Cardio allows for capillary growth and penetration into muscle that is being developed. Cardio, then, is a significant part of the training process since it is the capillary blood vessels that will bring nutrients and energy to exercising muscle, as well as taking away the carbon dioxide, lactic acid, and other waste products from exercising muscle. Incorporating good regular cardio into workout regimens will help to prevent cramps.

SPRAINS AND STRAINS

Sprains and strains are two different things. A sprain involves a stretched or torn ligament, while a strain also involves a stretch or a tear but, in this case, of the muscle itself. Recognizing the condition is fairly easy, as is detecting the severity of the injury: in general, the more serious the sprain or strain, the harder it is to use the area where the injury is located. For example, is the patient slightly favoring the ankle, or is it simply impossible for her to put weight on the affected foot at all?

Physicians grade sprains on a scale of one to three. Grade one is a stretch or tear to a ligament that is relatively mild, and the affected joint shows little instability. Grade two is more severe, but the tear to the ligament is incomplete. Grade three is a completely ruptured ligament and is accompanied by instability that may be so severe that the patient can't use the limb at all. Milder sprains can be treated at home, but let your son or daughter's ability to use the affected limb, and his or her level of pain or discomfort, dictate whether a trip to the emergency room, the doctor, and perhaps an X-ray, is required to determine the extent of the injury or if there is an actual fracture.

Most sprains and strains can be treated by using *RICE* during the first 24-72 hours after the injury. RICE is an acronym for REST, ICE, COMPRESSION, and ELEVATION.

REST. Don't use the injured limb — don't put weight on an injured ankle or knee, hip or groin, and don't lift anything with an injured elbow or wrist — for the first 24-48 hours.

ICE. The right amount of cold constricts the veins, which helps to slow down the swelling and inflammation, and eases pain. Too much cold can actually cause or exacerbate the injury, so never place ice directly on the skin, and always limit your "ice on" time. Use an ice pack on the injured area for no longer than twenty minutes, and rest the area for at least half an hour before icing it again. Usually two to three days of ice on/ice off is sufficient to heal a mild injury.

COMPRESSION. Like ice, compression can help to reduce swelling. Wrap the injured area in an elastic bandage or compression sleeve. It's important to make sure that it's not too compressed. If fluid can't flow out of the injured area, swelling will worsen, not improve.

ELEVATION. To keep fluid from accumulating in the injured area, and decrease swelling, rest the injured area on a pillow that's elevated above the patient's heart.

I also recommend a rather stinky therapy for swelling: an onion poultice. I warn you that the odor isn't pleasant, but it really puts out the inflammatory fire.

Take four medium raw onions, chopped medium, and when it's time to place the poultice on the body, mix them with one half cup of coarse sea salt. Pack the onions around the swollen area and wrap it all up securely with Saran wrap. Place two or three big beach towels, a waterproof sheet, or an old shower curtain underneath the wrapped area — between the injury and the table the injured arm or the sofa the injured leg is resting upon — because what is going to happen is that the onions are going to draw the fluid right out of the swollen area. It's an old time sort of remedy — the healing power of onions — but it works. To quote Eugene, "It stinks but, damn, it feels better." A generous wash with lemon juice after an hour-long poultice helps to neutralize that stink.

As for supplements, curcumin, a spice derived from the turmeric plant, is a powerful natural anti-inflammatory agent that you can purchase in many health food stores and compounding pharmacies as a supplement. Find a brand that contains bioperine, which is an alkaloid made from the fruits of black pepper, as an ingredient, or take a black pepper extract supplement with the curcumin, as bioperine potentiates the effects of curcumin. The recommended dosage of curcumin is 500 mg every few hours while the swelling lasts. Side effects — nausea, dizziness, and diarrhea — are rare and minimal.

I also like a product called CH-Alpha, a liquid, over-the-counter supplement that contains collagen hydrolysate, which is beneficial in rebuilding damaged cartilage. For children over twelve, one vial daily until the flexibility of the joint returns to normal should help tremendously. For my professional athletes, or folks with repetitive use issues, like runners, I like to use CH-Alpha prophylactically. Side effects — diarrhea and flatulence — are again rare and almost always minimal.

These simple therapies should alleviate Grade one and Grade two sprains within about three days. However, sometimes it will seem as if a sprain or a strain is healing, but then the pain grows more severe. This may mean that the injury is more complicated or involved than a simple strain or sprain. If the swelling doesn't decrease, and the pain doesn't subside substantially within 72 hours, go see a doctor.

For more severe injuries, follow your doctor's advice for rehabilitation, of course. In general, however, you want to walk a fine line between rushing back into action and babying the injury too much — put weight on the injured area too soon and you run the risk of reinjury; stay immobile for too long and the area can cause scar tissue to form and allow muscles to weaken, and that can lead to difficulty with mobility when you do try to use the area again. Start slowly to rebuild strength, and let your child's comfort level determine how far to push. There is almost always some discomfort when you begin to use a sprained or strained area again, but keep in mind that *acute* pain is a signal of a setback and more RICE is in order.

CONCUSSIONS

Probably the injury that has the most dire long-term effects is getting hit on the head. We have for too long written off the head blows our children sustain at play with euphemisms like "he got his bell rung" or "she got beamed in the brain." Let's call it was it really is: a brain injury. Perhaps a mild one but, nonetheless, every blow to the head causes some form of damage to the brain.

We've already talked about the symptoms — disorientation, dizziness, blurred vision, headache, problems with balance, difficulty concentrating, nausea. And we've already noted, though it bears repeating: *a concussion does not necessarily involve a loss of consciousness.* Most of us associate concussions with contact sports like boxing, football, hockey, and soccer. But a baseball pitch hits your son in the forehead, or your daughter falls off the high beam and thumps her head on the gym floor, and you may have a concussion to deal with. If it happens enough times, that's called *multiple concussions*, which are more likely to cause permanent damage than a single, isolated incident.

The standard treatment for a concussion involves resting — *without the visual stimulation of screens* — and perhaps taking an over-the-counter pain relief medicine[1]. If the concussion is severe enough, your doctor or coach will likely recommend that your kid stops playing contact sports for a few days, and sometimes up to a few months. That's because returning to the game before a first concussion is healed could result in *second impact syndrome*, in which the brain swells rapidly after a second concussion before the symptoms from the first one have abated. And that is a potentially fatal condition.

Let me take this opportunity to dispel a myth, and offer two newer, and more effective, treatment methods for concussions.

The myth: you shouldn't go to sleep with a concussion. A concussion is a condition that can but does not necessarily involve a loss of consciousness — but it does *not* involve internal bleeding. The guidelines for a good night's rest after a concussion are a matter of *unless*, and *until*, *if* and *about*: *unless* your child's doctor has indicated further treatment is necessary, and *until* his symptoms have abated, and *if* he is able to sit up and have a normal conversation, then he'll likely want to go to sleep and you should let him, with

---

1 It is worth saying here that there are basically two types of over-the-counter pain medications- acetaminophen, and all of the other things we think of as NSAIDS- most common of which is ibuprofen. More and more often the medical field is realizing that acetaminophen has been grossly overused at great risk to the liver. But especially, when we are talking about an injured brain, it's critical to understand that an injured brain needs an extraordinary supply of glutathione to heal. Acetaminophen inhibits glutathione synthesis, so probably is not the best choice for pain relief when the brain is the source of pain. Ibuprofen and other related NSAIDS can, with prolonged use, increase the risk of bleeding, so use it only for short periods of time.

the caveat that you should check on him *about* every two hours during the first twenty-four hours following the concussion incident.

The new and effective treatment methods are: the medication L-methylfolate, Vitamin B6, and hyperbaric therapy.

There are many forms of L-methylfolate out there. They are not all created equally, and their dose per capsule or pill varies widely. The FDA has insisted that physicians monitor folate consumption as it can mask a B-12 deficiency if taken in large doses — an issue that brings us back to the importance of data gathering, including blood work if indicated, with that annual well visit to the doctor. I often choose CerefolinNAC as the methylfolate source for my athletes. It is a prescription-only form of L-methylfolate combined with N-acetylcysteine and methyl B-12 that is not, despite its prescription status, usually covered by insurance. Folic acid is necessary to prevent heart disease, stroke, and vascular disease. As the body metabolizes folic acid, it takes on a form that assists in manufacturing DNA. Further along the metabolic pathway, it becomes L-methylfolate, a crucial participant in the function of our body's neurotransmitters, those biochemicals by which our brain cells communicate with each other across synapses. By increasing the amount of activated folic acid in the system when the body is recovering from a concussion, we give our kids a powerful tool to facilitate the brain's function.

Where Vitamin B6 can be helpful is with the generation of new nerve growth once a neural sheer occurs. When a neural connection breaks, there are consequences for connections beyond the one that is broken. To understand what I mean by this, let's say you broke a bone in your leg, the tibia, for example. The tibia is the larger, and stronger, bone in your lower leg, often referred to as the shinbone. When the shinbone is broken, the consequences of the injury aren't limited to just that bone, but to the knee, where the tibia forms one of two articulations with the femur, to the ankle where it connects and forms what is known as the talocrural joint, and to the hip which, though not directly connected to the tibia, can become weak, sore, and even atrophy during the time the tibia is in a cast, healing. This "cascade" or "domino" effect, wherein other bones and joints are impacted when one of them sustains an injury, happens in the brain too: when one neural network sustains an injury, the next and the next and the next one down the chain can also be impacted. The brain injury isn't isolated but, in this way, can become a chronic, progressive injury. Vitamin B6 is critical to the healthy construction of nerves and brain cells, as well as to helping those brain cells talk to each other properly and efficiently through neurotransmitter formation.[1] While this capacity is not yet settled science, I recommend that my football players take a generous dose of Vitamin B6 after they've taken a hit. The downside to taking Vitamin B6 — either a generous dose of it for a short period of time, or a moderate dose over an extended period — is generally not a great concern because B6 is water soluble, meaning that if you take too much of it, and your body can't use all that you've given it, you will simply pee it away. Vitamin B6 is available in capsule and tablet form, and the broccoli sprout extract I spoke about earlier in this section is also a good source.

Hyperbaric therapy, or hyperbaric oxygen therapy (HBOT) is, essentially, the medical use of plain, old oxygen, albeit under higher atmospheric pressure than is possible by simply breathing. I have successfully used it with my autistic patients, my injured NFL players, menopausal mothers

---

1   http://www.ncbi.nlm.nih.gov/pubmed/23517914.

and my elder patients who refer to it as "the fountain of youth." I routinely advise my young patients' parents, once we've screened and cleared them medically, to crawl into the chamber with their children at every possible opportunity as the therapy helps not only my young, primary patients, but their caregivers with stress modulation — and I suspect, since this is something I've observed over many years of use in my office, that it may decrease addictive drives for substances such as alcohol, tobacco, and other drugs. I cannot overstress the importance of screening and clearing patients for use of hyperbarics. While home units that are manufactured by a reputable company have been very carefully approved for use at home, they must still be prescribed for an individual by a physician who has ensured that the patient can safely use it.

The word hyperbaric means, literally, "high" (hyper) "pressure" (baric). And though just beginning to emerge in mainstream medicine as a go-to therapeutic tool for a variety of seemingly unrelated illnesses, the concept has been around for centuries. Its most likely father was a British clergyman named Henshaw who, in 1662, constructed an entire room to act as a chamber in which air pressure could be increased by use of an organ bellows. The increased air pressure, he believed, could help people who suffered from acute pulmonary, or lung-related, ailments, among other illnesses. This was the same year, it should be noted, that physicist and chemist Robert Boyle first published his law, known as Boyle's Law, describing the relationship between pressure and gas. Simply stated, Boyle discovered that pressure decreases the volume of gas or, in other words, condenses it. Henshaw's enormous hyperbaric "device," however, increased air pressure but did not directly increase the concentration of oxygen being supplied to the occupants. It wasn't until 1772 that chemists Carl Wilhelm Scheele, a Swede, and Joseph Priestly, an Englishman, isolated the element of oxygen and real advances in the science of hyperbarics began.

Over the centuries, in both Europe and North America, hyperbaric therapy was used to treat cholera, rickets, nervous disorders, diabetes, syphilis, and the victims of the Spanish Influenza epidemic that swept the United States at the close of WWI. It wasn't until the mid-1930s, however, when the use of hyperbarics proved effective in the treatment of decompression sickness in deep sea divers, that the U.S. military took notice of its benefits and its potential uses for military purposes. That's when the age of modern hyperbarics really began. What is exciting is that in recent years, there has been a tremendous amount of research on the use of hyperbarics for various types of traumatic brain injury, with excellent outcomes especially at lower pressure.[1] There continues to be some debate in the medical literature, mostly because it is often puzzling to folks that lower pressure might be as good or better than higher pressure. But what we keep finding is that the brain seems to prefer lower pressures. Overall the preponderance of the research is very favorable and my clinical experience with hyperbarics has been phenomenal over the years.

Hyperbaric therapy is based on a simple fact: breathing — *air* — is essential to life. We breathe because cells that are deprived of oxygen will die. Normally, however, the air that we breathe is composed of about 21% oxygen. Modern hyperbarics works by allowing us to breathe up to 100% oxygen, both condensing the gas and pressurizing it so that it penetrates our blood stream at a much higher and faster rate than is possible in any other circumstance.

---

1 http://online.liebertpub.com/doi/abs/10.1089/neu.2011.1895.

In our blood stream, the oxygen binds to the hemoglobin in our red blood cells, which is the standard way the element is carried to our tissues and organs. However, when under pressure, oxygen also dissolves into our plasma. Plasma is the thin, yellowish fluid in which our blood cells are transported throughout the body, carrying air and nutrients and other life-giving essentials to all the rest of our cells. This dissolved oxygen — which hyperbarics has made so much more plentiful in the blood stream — can penetrate deep into our tissues and organs, flooding damaged cells, like a tsunami wave, with the healing element.

Flooding the brains of children who have cerebral palsy with oxygen has been shown to reawaken dormant areas of the brain,[2] — and by the same principle, hyperbarics may offer new hope for stroke victims, no matter how long ago their strokes may have occurred.[3] Flooding the injuries of my bruised and battered NFL players with oxygen after a game has reduced inflammation and swelling as well as the actual physical appearance of hematomas as the extra oxygen breaks down the unsightly bruise itself and carries away the crusted blood and other cells via the blood stream. Flooding my autistic patients with oxygen, of course, seems to improve every system in their little bodies — improving immune function, facilitating digestions and improving other gut problems, and helping to clear the "autistic fog" that makes them appear as if their intellectual and emotional capacities are lesser than those of neurotypical children; in short, addressing and improving, simultaneously and painlessly, every symptom of autism.

When it comes to brain injuries, flooding the brain with oxygen helps the body to repair the neurons that

2 http://www.thelancet.com/journals/lancet/article/PIIS0140-6736(00)05136_9/fulltext.
3 http:www.calgaryhyperbariccentre.com/docs/Hyperbaric_Oxygenation_Adjunct_Therapy_in_Strokes_due_
    to_Thrombosis.pdf.

experienced neural sheer when the head took the blow, literally restoring the pathways where our knowledge, memories, and understanding of the world around us are stored.

All that said, I want to draw a clear distinction between what we are talking about in this section — hyperbaric therapy, or HBOT — and other forms of "oxygen therapy." In HBOT, the patient essentially takes a leisurely nap in — or, at low pressures, even spends the night sleeping comfortably in — an enclosed chamber filled with pressurized air. The chamber is about the same dimensions as the lower bunk in a set of bunk beds, and the downsides are few:

- Transient discomfort in the ears or sinuses may be felt by some people as the chamber comes up to pressure, similar to the way some people feel in a plane upon takeoff or landing. This is easily countered by the same tricks that fliers and divers employ to equalize their eardrums — swallowing, or holding the nose and blowing gently. There should never be continued pain while pressurizing in a hyperbaric chamber. Ears must clear, just as they must when flying or scuba diving.
- Perfumes or colognes should not be worn into the chamber as the scents, pleasant enough in a normal atmosphere, can become quite intense and often unpleasant under pressure.
- A trip to the bathroom before a dive into the hyperbaric chamber is essential. The pressure in the "tank" helps all of the fluids that accumulate in your legs during the day to go straight to your kidneys, filling your bladder in a hurry. I often try to put my feet up for an hour before getting in the chamber for

the evening, hoping to make it for as long as possible before I've got to go to the bathroom.

♦ Chilliness can be a factor inside the chamber — not cold, but crisp — if there's a lot of air circulating around the compressors, and so I always make sure I take a nice, soft blanket in with me. Conversely, if there is insufficient circulating cooler air around the compressors that make a chamber work, it can get warm in a chamber.

There are a few circumstances under which you or your child may want or need to avoid HBOT. Pregnant women have been advised to forego hyperbarics, more because there isn't published research on its use in this situation than because it's known to be a risk or a problem. In fact, there is a clear consensus that it *should* be used if a person suffers smoke inhalation and carbon monoxide exposure, pregnant or not. Insulin-dependent diabetics must monitor their sugars very carefully when using hyperbarics — we know that blood sugars drop significantly while in a hyperbaric chamber and can lead to hypoglycemic seizures if the user isn't appropriately cautious. Also, anyone who has had a recent pneumothorax should avoid chamber use. My textbook said that those taking certain drugs such as Antabuse for the treatment of alcoholism should not use hyperbarics, although I've never found an explanation of why this might be. For cancer patients, there have been, additionally, discussions about avoiding hyperbarics while receiving radiation, and when certain chemotherapeutic agents, such as Adriamycin and Cisplatin, are being used. This is not because of known drug interactions or unacceptable side effects, but because the mode of action of these particular treatments is more or less "opposite" to the mode of action of oxygen in the body, and the assumption was made that they probably shouldn't be used together. It was, however, also suggested that, at the least, hyperbarics can safely be resumed when the course of radiation or chemotherapy is complete.

"Oxygen therapy" can simply mean breathing in oxygen while sitting around in a hospital or the sidelines of a game. It can also refer to ozone therapy, something that is quite a bit different from HBOT. That is generally an invasive procedure in which hydrogen peroxide or ozone is introduced into the body by way of injection into muscle tissue or blood stream — in some cases through the rectum or vagina. Such therapies are still considered controversial by many in the medical field, but it is being studied more and more with some excellent outcomes. Ozone therapy is, in any case, not appropriate for children at the time of this writing.

What you want to look for in a hyperbaric therapy facility is one that offers *low-pressure* hyperbaric chambers, or "mild personal" or "soft shell" hyperbaric chambers. High-pressure chambers, the original design and function of the therapy, are hard-shelled, made of metal, deliver oxygen under an amount of pressure that can itself be stressful to the body, and the sessions can be terribly expensive — around $1200 per hour! Advancements in the understanding of how hyperbarics works have led to the development of low-pressure, soft-sided chambers, such as the ones I use in my office and have at home. These personal chambers, when inflated, look like a long tube and are about the width of a camp cot. They fit one large offensive lineman or extra large basketball player comfortably — and are ideal for parent and child! — delivering life-giving oxygen at a pressure that nourishes and heals the body's tissues, all at an average cost of about $100 per hour.

Please see the Resources section at the end of this book for help in finding a hyperbaric therapy facility near you, or to rent or purchase your own hyperbaric chamber for in-home use.

*"*You can't prove prevention.*"*

Julie has covered hyperbarics pretty thoroughly, but I have a few thoughts to add. For one thing, I know that I'm not as rundown as I would be at the end of the season because I often sleep in a hyperbaric chamber. Sometimes I spend the whole night in the chamber, and sometimes only three and a half or four hours, but I do get some time in every night.

I do this because I know it is important to my long-term health and brain function — my ability to be a good husband and father, and my ability to do my job. I take a lot of hits in each game I play, and I want to heal the injuries that result — bruises, sprains, and any neuronal sheers that have to be repaired because I've suffered a concussion — as quickly and efficiently as possible.

I also know that however important hyperbaric therapy is — and how *critical* it is in healing any damage done by concussions — it can be prohibitive in terms of the family budget. I keep trying to think of ways that this amazing tool can be made more widely available to young athletes everywhere, keeping in mind that Julie is fierce about needing to have the use of hyperbarics appropriately prescribed and supervised.

Conclusion

"I thrive in the NFL thanks, in great part, to my wife, Nureya."

Believe me, what I just said isn't just lip service.

Life in the NFL comes with thrills and perks, of course, but it also comes with obligations that I have to imagine are awfully daunting for the guys who don't have a supportive family to come home to.

I have a pretty serious work ethic. I believe all those clichés about reaping what you sow and getting out only what you put in, but actually, actively doing all the little things every day that will add up to the big thing — you know, like taking a pass on the sticky bun because while you know it might taste good in the moment, it will also make you feel like crap the next day — that can be hard. It's easier to make the choices minute by minute to exercise the discipline I need to be my best because my wife has an incredibly substantial work ethic, too. And she doesn't just back up my own better instincts, she lives them with me. After a win, for example, there may be a dozen or more family members waiting for me to celebrate, but she gets that taking care of my body, so that I can help my team win the next week, too, is simply a part of my job. There's never pressure to rush to the family celebration — I take the half an hour for my post-game IV with complete peace of mind.

But, of course, that's not the way it goes just in the NFL. A supportive family enhances the thrills and perks in every walk, and aspect, of life — including that of a young athlete. But you get that — that's why you're reading this book: you're a smart, supportive parent who wants to have all the information you need to care for your kid in the healthiest and most proactive way possible.

So let me go back to something Julie and I talked about earlier in this book. That is, most of our kids — your kids, and my kids — are unlikely to have a career at the most elite level of sport. But that's not really why we want our kids on the field or the court or the mat anyway. We encourage our kids to play sports and be active because, well, first of all, because its *fun*. And it gives them a sense of community. It teaches them discipline and hones their own budding work ethic. It provides them with the exercise they need to build a foundation for a lifetime of overall good health.

I grant you that some of the changes we're recommending in this book may be difficult, at first. It's never easy to make adjustments to parts of our lives as significant and intimate as the way we eat, or to shift a lifetime of thinking in one way about health to another. I know first hand that it isn't easy. Nureya and I *still* kid each other that, before we met Julie and took to heart what she had to teach us, we thought that eating at Boston Market was a healthier choice than picking up a pizza for the family dinner.

But I will promise you this. Once you experience the results of the shift — how much better you will feel, how much more energy you will have, how much healthier it is possible to be — all you and your kids will want is more.

Eugene Monroe
March 2016

About the Authors

JULIE A. BUCKLEY, MD, is the author of *Healing Our Autistic Children: A Medical Plan for Restoring Your Child's Health* and *Breast Cancer: Start Here*. She practices functional medicine in Ponte Vedra Beach, Florida (*www.pppvonline.com*) where she lives with her husband and two children.

As a senior at the University of Virginia, EUGENE MONROE was a Unanimous All-ACC selection, and voted top blocker in the conference. He was drafted eighth overall in the 2009 NFL Draft by the Jacksonville Jaguars where, in 2010, he helped the Jags rank third in the NFL with 149.7 rushing yards per game. In 2013, the Super Bowl Champion Baltimore Ravens orchestrated a trade to acquire this star left tackle. In his short time as a Raven, Eugene has been consistently graded as one of the best pass blockers in the NFL. Every summer, Eugene hosts the Eugene Monroe All Pro Football Camp, a free camp experience for kids who want to learn how to improve the fundamentals of their game. Eugene also owns 4th Down Partners, a real estate development company based in Maryland, where he lives with his wife and two children.

Resources

FUNCTIONAL MEDICINE

To find a functional medicine practitioner near you, your best bet is to go right to the source, The Institute for Functional Medicine at *www.functionalmedicine.org*.

HYPERBARICS

For more information about buying or renting a hyperbaric unit — or to find a hyperbaric facility near you — go to *http://www.hyperbaricphp.com*.

NUTRITION

Rebecca Katz, a trained chef who holds a Masters of Science degree in Health and Nutrition Education, cooks up some awesome stuff your family will love. Visit her at *http://www.rebeccakatz.com*.

Yummy meals from Jessica Seinfeld's cookbooks, *Deceptively Delicious: Simple Secrets to Get Your Kids Eating Good Food* and *Double Delicious: Simple Food for Busy, Complicated Lives*, are staples from my kitchen.

GFCF Recipes for Gluten-free and Casein-free Diets and Basic Recipes for the Beginning Cook comes from Pat Buckley, a long-time home-ec teacher and my mom, who stepped right up to learn how to cook gluten- and casein-free for my family. The book is not entirely GFCF recipes, but teaches you how to work on converting recipes you have and love.

Cooking, for me, is a creative and relaxing activity, and I find myself on the Internet — often at *www.foodnetwork.com*, *www.allrecipes.com* or on Pinterest — scouting for recipes to surprise and please my family. When the recipes call for ingredients that aren't part of the gluten- and casein-free diet my family follows, I find it pretty darned easy to make substitutions — but my family has been eating GFCF diet for years so I'm very familiar with it. For those of you who are interested in reading more about the GFCF diet, *www.gfcfdiet.com* is a good place to start.

Don't forget to be aware of what foods are so important to consume organically. "The Dirty Dozen Clean Fifteen" list is updated annually at *www.ewg.org*.

SUPPLEMENTS

The quality of the supplements you give to your family is key. You want to make sure the ones you're buying haven't been sitting around in the warehouse of a large distributor or big box store losing their potency — or, worse, becoming oxidized so taking them is worse for you than if you took no dietary supplements at all.

Good places to find quality supplements are your local compounding pharmacy, or your hometown's organic or whole food market. Many good brands, including the ones I recommend in these pages, are also widely available on the Internet. For the convenience of my patients, I maintain a supplement supply service; the service supports the Healthy U Now Foundation and can be accessed at *www.healthyustore.com*.

SLEEP CYCLE ALARM CALCULATOR

There are several apps and web sites that can provide this information — here's one of them: *http://sleepyti.me*.